THREATS AGAINST THE BREEDER

PREGNANT WITH FOUR ALPHAS' BABIES

BOOK THREE

BELLA MOONDRAGON

OLIVIA BHELLE KILDARE

ROGUE WOLF PUBLISHING

For our pets

CONTENTS

CHAPTER 1: FINDING OUT THE FATHER

Rose

I've watched a talk show before where the mother is adamantly stating to the host who the father of the child is. When the presenter reads the results and declares, "You are NOT the father," the majority of those women invariably get the shock of their life. For me today, the doctor's office resembles that program, somewhat, but without the crowd, cameras, and glamorous lighting.

Well, scratch the no audience bit as the four Alphas, Kelly, and Shelby all sit with me as we wait for instructions from the doctor on what happens next. We have a full crowd today.

The palace clinic usually smells like disinfectant, but today the smell seems a bit more pungent and is making my eyes water and my heart race… maybe it is the nerves.

"What if the results say none of the Alphas are the father? What if the doctor says I have four panfish or trout swimming in there instead?" I whisper to Shelby and Kelly leans over to hear what we are discussing.

They both jerk their heads back simultaneously and stare at me. A crease forms between Shelby's eyebrows before she shakes her head a little.

"Honey, unless you are a mermaid of some kind, I don't know how you would be carrying fish in there," Shelby says.

"I had sex with Eli in a lake once.... What if some fishies you know... swam in there?" I mutter in hushed tones.

"Firstly, ew! I really didn't have to hear that about my brother. I know he has sex, but now I just got a mental picture of the actual deed. Secondly, it doesn't work like that. The only animals your babies will shift into are gorgeous pups."

"Or tadpoles," I whisper.

The Alphas are all pacing up and down. They at times bump into each other, and their uncoordinated nervous movements are making my head spin and causing my anxiety to hit an all-time high.

One of the Alphas, or more, has to be the father, right? I was a thousand percent sure, but that television program is causing doubts to float to the surface like oil in water.

And what would happen to the Alphas who weren't the fathers? Did it mean they would stop caring for me? Would they abandon me and return to their packs? I really didn't want to lose any of my Alphas... not now when I was getting to spend some time with them again.

Dr. Pendergoober makes her way in with a nurse I have never seen before. She sits behind the huge executive desk and peers at me from above the rims of her glasses.

"How are you doing today?" she asks plainly.

"Like I have fish swimming in my belly," I answer.

"You're fourteen weeks pregnant, a bit too early to be feeling the babies move or kick. That is probably your uterus expanding to accommodate the growing babies. It could feel like fish swimming, yes." Was this the doctor's take on dry humor?

Kelly puts a hand to her mouth as she tries to muffle a laugh.

"Well, I think Rose thinks she has literal fish swimming in her womb," Shelby interjects.

This time everyone in the room turns to look at me. I can feel my face warming up. Did Shelby have to announce that? I didn't want everyone in the room to know I'd been joking about a fish impregnating me. Of course, I didn't really think that. I was just voicing my concerns in the most ridiculous way possible.

"Even if you have been eating too much fish, that won't turn your babies into a sea creature," Dr. Pendergong clarifies.

I open my mouth to clarify but decide to let it go. I will let her think I am stupid enough to think whatever food I eat is what my babies will turn into. If that were the case, I would be carrying little peanut babies... or tiny cucumbers with peanuts for eyes.

I laugh as I imagine what it would be like if a fish really were the father. How would I ever find that singular fish in a lake with so many other fish to give it the good news about its pending fatherhood? The doctor pulls me from my thoughts.

"We will be performing a non-invasive and risk-free prenatal paternity test. We took a simple blood draw sample from Rose and a buccal mouth swab sample from the four Alphas. Analysis was done on the cell-free fetal DNA found in the mother's blood and compared to the samples provided by the Alphas," Dr. Pendergonad is saying.

I blink as my brain is trying to follow all the medical jargon that is coming out of her mouth. So far, all I know is she said something about DNA and blood.

"Excuse me, Doc, would you mind speaking in simplified English? Not that I am not intelligent enough to understand medical terms or anything, but please, just for the benefit of my fellow Alphas here," Tristan requests.

I giggle, although my heart is racing at this point.

"I will try. Using state-of-the-art technology, we were able to isolate the fetal DNA from the maternal blood plasma and analyze 300,000 genetic markers to establish paternity. We were then able to accurately confirm or exclude paternity," the doctor continues.

I can't help but gape at her, wondering if that was her version of simplified English. No wonder studying medicine took endless years. These people had to actually learn a new language before even learning anything about medicine.

"Who is the father or fathers, doctor?" Shelby asks, cutting through the medical jargon. I hope the doctor will just give the answer without diving deeper into the whole plasma business again.

Were there sharks in the lake? That would be poetic right? I would be a mommy shark, carrying the live version of a baby shark. I would be on televisions then, answering questions from journalists. Maybe even get my own reality show where the theme song would be, 'Baby Shark.'

Dr. Pendergogo proceeds to flip through some pages in a folder the nurse hands to her.

"You have two sets of heteropaternal superfecundation twins," she announces.

"Doc, English please," Tristan says in an annoyed tone.

"Each child has different genetic markers. Each of them matches the different Alphas."

This time I roll my eyes. This wasn't a television show, and there was no need to build tension or cliffhangers to engage the audience. I needed her to spell it out for me.

"So who is the father? We all slept with her. Could our DNA have mixed inside her and become some kind of cocktail, and you can't tell who the father is because of that?" Reece asks.

Good question, I thought to myself.

This time the doctor laughs lightly. So she does have a sense of humor. "That isn't possible. Each child has a different father. Congratulations to the four of you. You are all going to be fathers."

I can feel my heart slow down and then race again. Had I heard her correctly? All my Alphas had scored?

Mark air punches and mutters a triumphant, "Yes!" Reece laughs and runs his hands in his hair. Tristan and Eli high-five and do a little synced dance routine, which ends in a funny twerk.

Shelby and Kelly both hold one of my hands. I look at Shelby, and she smiles at me.

"I am going to be an aunt!" Kelly cheers and lays her other hand on my belly.

"Yep. If any of the babies come out looking like a tiny fire hydrant, that's Eli's," Tristan adds.

4

"What are you talking about?" the doctor asks, but no one answers as the Alphas are celebrating and giving each other brotherly hugs paired with heavy back-patting. She doesn't know how silly these men can be.

"Congratulations, my friend," Shelby says and softly touches her forehead to mine.

"Yeah. I think the fish daddy you were talking about must have shot blanks... you know... down there," Shelby jokes and the three of us laugh.

I place a hand on my belly and feel a warm wave rush through me. I am carrying four children from the four men I love. I won't have to choose, and none of them will have to leave the palace.

We will all be able to raise our ch–

My happiness subsides immediately as I'm reminded that these children are still going to be taken by Emily.

My four babies from my four Alphas are going to be snatched away from me and handed to that monster; That murderer will be the one to raise my babies, who were created out of love, something she doesn't have a single ounce of in her whole demon body!

A deep sadness quickly replaces the warm feeling. As I raise my eyes, they meet Mark's gaze.

He smiles and mouths, "Are you okay?" I feign a smile and nod at him.

He raises one eyebrow, and I know he isn't buying my happy mommy act.

CHAPTER 2: A CONUNDRUM WITH THE DNA

ADAM

The king paces around looking like an angry Oompa Loompa as he listens to what Dr. Pendergan is telling him. His face has started to resemble an overripe tomato with every word the doctor utters.

"What do you mean all of them are the fathers? This wasn't what we agreed on!"

The doctor looks as taken aback as I am by that. It's as though he is accusing her of inseminating Rose with seed from all the Alphas.

"This is actually possible in biology and medical history, Your Majesty. There was a high possibility she could end up having multiple babies because of her double uterine horn," the doctor says.

He stomps his feet in anger. "You didn't warn me about this, doctor. You said a double-horned uterus was the best at getting pregnant quicker, not that it was some suction device sucking in every man's semen like a vacuum to create offspring. Could the DNA test be wrong?"

"The test is ninety-nine percent accurate," the doctor responds plainly.

"Well, maybe that one percent is worth looking into. They can't all be the fathers. There has to be one winner."

The doctor shrugs. No medical theory she can spin will change this.

"It appears the Moon Goddess had other plans then," the doctor iterates.

I smile secretly at her response. When medical reasoning fails, turn to mystical alternatives for answers.

"Could we terminate the other three babies before they are born?"

I feel the small hairs on my neck standing on end at this question. Was the king just pure evil? Kill the babies before they are even born? Emily had thought the only way to get rid of her problems was by killing, and now the king is thinking the same way.... Well, he is already thinking of killing Rose once the babies are born anyway. Is murder a family DNA trait that runs in their blood?

"With all due respect, Your Majesty, that will just endanger all of the babies. Doing that would result in her losing all the children... and even her life. I also doubt the Alphas would agree to have their children killed," Dr. Pendergan reasons.

I frown, wondering how he would even pick which of the four babies to kill. Would it be a game of Russian roulette? Three bullets, and the lucky one is the baby who will get the blank bullet? This man is crazy.

"Leave!" he barks, and the doctor curtsies and walks out.

"What are we going to do? The doctor thinks I am worried about the life of that Breeder. If getting rid of those babies kills her, who cares? Her days are numbered anyway. It would make your job of killing her that much easier. We could always find another Breeder. She's replaceable." He is talking to me.

"The Alphas would never agree to such an act. They will fight you, Your Majesty, if you mess with the lives of their children. This is bigger than just getting rid of the Breeder. Bigger than the throne as well. What she is carrying within her is their blood, and fathers will go to extremes to protect their young ones," I say as forcefully as I can.

He snorts and stops to look at me. "There can't be four kings.

Emily can't marry all four of them. There has to be one winner, and you will come up with a better plan for that to happen."

I swallow nervously. I know he has always believed me to be weak and stupid, and he never admits that I am always the one to come up with most of 'his' brilliant plans.

"I think we shouldn't act hastily—" I begin, but he cuts me off.

"Maybe I should have just let Alpha Kane be king. This whole nonsense would have been avoided." Then he mutters, "Maybe I shouldn't abdicate the throne at all."

I am not sure what to make of that last remark, so I ignore it. "Well, I think it's a little late for 'should haves,' Your Majesty. I also doubt you would have been willing to let your beautiful cousin Emily marry Alpha Kane." I want to high-five myself for managing to keep a straight face while saying the words 'beautiful' and 'Emily' in the same sentence.

"You are right. But we need to have a solution, or I will call off this whole challenge."

"What if we continue with the challenge? When the Breeder is ready to have the babies, the first male child to come out of her will determine the winner," I suggest.

"What do you mean the first male child to come out will determine the winner? Babies don't talk, and I won't wait for it to grow up and then announce who the winner will be."

For a man most people label as wise and knowledgeable, the king is really unbelievably stupid.

I clear my throat and try again. "The father of the first male child to be born amongst the four children will be the king," I clarify.

"Ohhh! That's an awesome idea. That's how it will be then. I will tell the Alphas that the father of the first male child to be born amongst the four babies will be the king. Do you see why I am king, Beta Adam?"

Had the guy just taken credit for my idea again? And now he was asking me to stroke his ego by declaring him an awesome king?

"Yes, Your Majesty. Everyone knows there is no situation you can't handle."

Prick!

~

SHELBY

When Adam walks into our bed chambers, I am sitting by the window in a rocking chair. I can't help but smile as I watch some robins playing in the garden fountain outside.

I turn around, get up, and walk toward him as he enters.

"Well...? What is the king going to do now that all four Alphas are the fathers?"

"He wanted to kill three of the babies," he says.

"What is with him and his cousin always wanting to kill everyone?" I can't believe what I'm hearing.

"Don't worry, I talked him out of that madness. I also talked him out of calling the challenge off," he responds.

"So they will all be kings?" I feel my eyes grow wider as I imagine if that could be a possibility.

"No. I came up with a plan he accepted. The father of the first male child born will be king."

"Oh...that's sexist, isn't it? What if all four children are girls?" I shrug. Trust me to always have questions for my man's brilliant ideas.

"Well, then we will think of another plan. Maybe the father of the most masculine-looking baby girl will be king then," he defends himself, sounding a little annoyed.

"Aww, don't be angry, my love. I'm proud of you for managing to keep this challenge going and for saving those children. Don't mind my forever racing mind. If all the children are girls, we'll cross that bridge when we come to it. For now, my man saved the day. And I want to show you just how much I appreciate and am proud of you." I give him a mischievous smile and step back.

I know the king will be looking for him soon, and I know we might not have enough time for a full tumble in the sheets session, so to speak.

"Baby, I don't think we have time for that. Not now anyway, maybe later," he replies. Really, he's turning this joyous opportunity down?

"This won't take that long." I wink at him and pull some pins from my hair, letting it free.

I want to see him lose all control with me again. I want to see him as wild as he was on our honeymoon night. I kneel in front of him.

It has been a while since I have given my man head. This married life can make one overlook the pleasures of giving joy in other ways than the traditional sense.

He looks down at me, and there is no mistaking the pure hunger in his gaze.

"Shel—"

"Shh!"

I run the palm of my hand over his trousers and feel his manhood leap to life. It feels hard and thick even from under the heavy cotton material of his pants.

Slowly, I pull down the zipper, and like an angry cobra ready to attack, his rod pounces out of the restrictive piece of clothing.

I can't help but marvel at the beauty of it. The veins coursing through its length look like dazzling finishing touches to perfection. His rod twitches and seems to grow harder from just my gaze, and I realize I've been gaping at it for some time now.

The milky liquid that is dripping from the mushroom head tells me that he is ripe for the harvest. I salivate as I think about how he will taste after all this time. I can hear him breathing heavily while struggling to maintain some sort of composure.

He's big; irreverent. Obscenely protruding out; intimidating. It's begging for a lick... demanding for one. I run my tongue along its length, the wet surface of my mouth teasing and activating the nerve ends of his veins. His pecker twitches again in response.

I wet my index finger with my tongue and softly drag it along the slit at the head, bringing wetness along his cock. After getting the entire head wet, I look up and catch his burning stare. Then, slowly, I lean in to blow air on the slicked skin... as if fanning the flames I have already ignited.

I can feel a pool forming in between my thighs and reach down in my pants with one hand. I let my finger rub away the pulsating need building inside my sensitive tissues.

I take his rigid shaft in my mouth with the other hand. I move my head forward and let the tip hit the far end of the back of my throat. My eyes roll back as I savor the taste…. I have missed this.

I hold back my gagging reflex with practiced ease and repeat the movement, but this time, I bring my inner cheeks in to create a vacuum motion. I taste the salty juice on my tongue and moan at the aphrodisiac effect it channels through my body. I incline my head to the side as I repeat the motion. Lapping, sucking, and tasting.

His orgasm is prompt, and with his release comes my own earth-shattering one. The volume of the intoxicating spasms coursing through my body is urged on by the flick of my wrist on my clit. Warm, rich liquid from his ejaculation gives me a deserved facial born of pure passion.

The jets go on and on. He doesn't take his hand to grab at his hungry flesh to try and ride it out. I bend down and nestle his balls on my tongue. A little suck on them causes him to stagger and shiver.

That release… those cries are for me. Only for me.

And he is still the most beautiful thing I've ever seen in all my years.

I lounge in the unadulterated animal femininity that flows through me in response to the picture of him. My own orgasms come in waves, making my body convulse in response to the gruff groans from my man that are beautiful like erotic musical notes to my ears.

This is what I am, what I have always been and had forgotten: a glutton for his pleasure. I live for it. My heart beats for it. I love it! I love him. I love us.

He looks around after it's over, seeming not to know what to do with himself.

"Thank you, my love. I am proud of you," I moan and lick my lips while our eyes stay locked.

Words are of no importance now as the raw desire is exchanged through our linked gazes that seem to promise each other a lot more passion to come.

CHAPTER 3: WHAT HAPPENS NEXT?

Mᴀʀᴋ

This room should stop being called Eli's room as it's become our meeting place. We may as well call it the common area now.

"Are you okay, baby?" I ask Rose, who is sitting with us in the room.

"Yeah," she responds and averts her eyes. Kelly whispers something to her, and they giggle.

"Care to share the joke?" Tristan prods.

"You wouldn't get the joke. It's a woman thing," Kelly says snidely.

I can see something is bothering Rose, but I am not sure this is the right time to be pushing her to divulge her fears. I hope to get a chance to talk to her alone soon. As I continue to look at her, I try to mentally visualize what a mix of our DNA will look like. I have no doubt our child will be adorable…. I have no uncertainty that any child she bears will be breathtaking. If any of the children resemble her, that will mean those children will be stunners.

"So what do you think will happen now that the four of us actually impregnated her?" Eli's voice cuts into my musings.

"That's a great question. Do you think the king will have no choice but to declare all four of us winners?" Tristan asks.

"Perhaps we could all share the throne. We have shown how we are able to share the most valuable prize with grace," Reece adds.

I shake my head and say, "Knowing the king, he will not allow that to happen."

"Then what will happen? Will he call off the challenge then?" Eli asks.

"I have no idea. All I know is that he has invested so much time into this whole thing already. Calling the challenge off would be stupid," Reece argues.

"Maybe Emily will just have to choose who she wants to marry amongst the four of us. I think she would pick Reece if that would be the case," Tristan teases.

Reece picks up a napkin and crumbles it before throwing it at Tristan. "Why would she choose me?"

"Because you are sooo cute–cute enough to eat. Be careful though, she might just literally eat you. That woman is evil, and I wouldn't put cannibalism past her," Tristan states.

We all laugh at this, but Reece doesn't seem to like being the butt of the joke. "I would rather jump off the nearest roof if she chooses me," I throw in.

"You are going to be a father, Reece. How can you be planning to go AWOL on your baby already? Some baby daddy you'll be," Tristan utters.

"Maybe she will choose you, Tristan. She looks like the kind of girl who enjoys a bit of 'S and M.' Agh, look at that. The two of you have something in common," Reece pushes back.

"Hell, no! I would never marry that witch even if she was the last woman on earth. I would rather be eaten alive by piranhas. Besides, I am already taken," Tristan says and winks at Rose. She in turn gives him a sweet smile that melts my heart. I realize then that I really miss her.

"We are all taken. The king will have to find another way to break the tie," I declare.

"You do realize whatever method he comes up with to solve this whole thing will still mean one of us will have to marry Emily?" Eli points out.

"I don't want to be the unlucky bastard. What would happen to the three of us who will end up not having the displeasure of being Emily's forever after?" Reece asks.

I shrug. "As long as we get to keep our children and Rose, I am fine with that."

"Y'all are idiots. The four of you might contend about keeping each of your children, but how do you think Rose feels?" Kelly asks.

We all turn and look at her. We exchange confused glances as she seems very irate, yet we all seem perplexed as to why.

"We don't mean any disrespect to Rose. I mean, what did we say that is wrong? We all love Rose and don't wish to be with any other person but her. What has gotten your thong in a fancy bow, my lady?" Tristan blurts out.

Kelly groans, reaches down, takes off her sandal, and throws it at him. I marvel at the way she aims as it would have hit him square on the mouth had he not moved slightly at the last second.

"You are such a jerk! I mean you would be okay keeping each of your children because all you have to lose is one child. Rose is the mother of all four; losing even one of those children will destroy her."

My heart races as I now understand why Rose is looking the way she does today. This is, granted, a celebratory moment, but for Rose, the pending notion of having to give up even one of her children to Emily is unimaginable.

I move forward and crouch in front of her. "You do know we will do all we can so that you don't lose any of your children?" I reassure her.

She looks at me, her eyes sparkling with unshed tears; they are laced with unmasked pain and fear of the uncertain future. I search the vocabulary in my head to try and find the right words to assure her of our loyalty to her and the children, but my word bank seems empty. I look up at the other three for help.

"Little flower, I will die before I let anyone take those children from you," Tristan confirms.

A tear rolls down her rosy cheek. I reach out to wipe it, and the sight of her tears undoes me.

"We will all fight to ensure you aren't separated from the children," Tristan continues.

"Will I be separated from any of you?" she asks in an almost whisper as her eyes dart to each of us in succession.

"As for me, it will take more than Kelly's impeccable aim with her shoe to separate me from you," Tristan announces and crouches beside me.

"I don't think you will get rid of any of us that easily, baby," I assure her, and the other men nod and hum their agreement.

"Even if she gives birth to four fish, right?" Kelly says. Rose sniffles and laughs. I look at Rose, wondering what this whole fish thing is about.

"I love you," Eli declares and sits on the couch's armrest next to Rose.

"Promise?" Rose asks.

"Promise!" Eli says proudly and picks up her hand before kissing the back of it.

"Everyone who loves Rose, say 'Aye'!" Tristan shouts.

"Aye!" we all chorus.

"Aye," Kelly shouts and leans over to give Rose a side hug.

"You promise your feelings for me won't change? Even if the babies can't shift into wolves? What if they shift into squirrels?" she ponders aloud.

"The chances of that happening are very slim, but I know we will love you and them either way. Even if they shift into Chihuahuas," I tease and she beams down at me.

I lean over and nuzzle her nose with my own. "We got you, baby."

"Thank you," she says, and I can hear her exhale ever so softly.

"Would any of you care for a snack? To show your support for the mother of your children, how do pickles and peanut butter sound?" Kelly asks.

We all give her hard stares. I wasn't about to eat that foul food combination before and can't do it now.

"Nope, I'm full." Eli is the first to respond. We all start coming up with one excuse or the other about why we can't eat the offered snack.

"You do know it's because of y'all's babies the poor girl is eating that? The least you could do is show your support," Kelly declares.

"I think I am allergic to peanuts," Eli exclaims.

"No, you're not, brother," she challenges.

"Shh!" Reece says.

"You aren't getting out of this that easily," Kelly scolds.

"No, it's not that. I think there is someone at the door."

We all get quiet so we can hear. The sound of shallow breathing and then faint rustling just outside the door hits our ears. It seems someone has been eavesdropping on our conversation.

I jump to my feet and head for the door. I storm into the hallway and see Emily's hastily retreating form. The witch!

Without a second thought, I follow her. I think it's time I had a word with 'Queen Grimhilde.'

CHAPTER 4: ALL IN

EMILY

I rush down the hallway, flying as fast as I can, trying not to lose my footing on the slick floor. I have to get back to my room unseen, but I'm afraid it's already too late, and someone knows I was hanging out around Eli's door.

I reach my room and tug on the doorknob only to stop at the sound of my name being shouted down the hallway after me.

"Emily!"

I spin around and see Alpha Mark coming after me. He is walking quickly, with a purpose, and even from a hundred feet away, I can see his nostrils flaring. He's obviously angry.

"Oh, Mark," I say, turning to face him. "Thank goodness you're here. I just ran out of my room. A huge mouse was in there, giant even! Have you seen Mr. Whiskers? Or perhaps you could kill it for me? Would you like to come inside?" I'm hinting that I mean inside of more than just my room.

Mark stands across from me, his arms folded in front of his massive chest. "Don't bullshit me, Emily," he says. "I know you were listening to our private conversation."

"What private conversation?" I flutter my eyelashes at him, pretending I don't know what he's talking about.

"The private conversation the four of us Alphas were having," he replies.

"Don't be silly!" I declare. "I didn't even know the four of you were in Eli's room."

He shakes his head at me. "Who said anything about Eli's room?"

I've been caught in a lie, and now I have to find a way to back out of it. "Well, don't you guys always sit in Eli's room to talk?"

"I know you were outside the door, Emily. We heard you breathing." He takes a few steps forward.

I back against the door, bracing my hands against the solid wood as I breathe in such a way that makes my bosom rise and fall above the low neckline of my elegant blue dress. I look extremely fetching in this particular gown, and I know it. I see his eyes lower and feel his heavy gaze on my breasts.

Perhaps I can take advantage of this situation. After all, I have an Alpha all to myself, near my room, and I know things he only dreams of knowing....

"What are you going to do, big boy?" I ask him, looking at him out of the corner of my eye as I turn my face to the side. "Spank me?"

He wrinkles up his nose. "No! But I was thinking of sending you the name of my tailor. You really should do something about the awful fit of that dress. If you paid someone to alter it for you, they did a terrible job. Practically everything is hanging out the top!"

He acts as if he's never seen breasts before, but then I recall that Rose is rather flat-chested.

I sigh and take my hands off of the door. "Listen, Mark, here's the deal," I begin. "I know something that you want to know. And if you want to know what I know you want to know, then you'll get to know me better. Do you know what I mean?"

The Alpha stares at me for a long moment and then asks, "What?"

Shaking my head, I push my door open. "Come in here for a moment so I can talk to you about that bi–Breeder." I decide perhaps it's better not to call her what I want to call her.

He follows me into my room, but I can tell he's reluctant to do so. "What do you want to tell me about Rose?" he demands.

I take a deep breath and stand in front of him with my hands folded in front of me like I'm about to sing at the Moon Goddess' temple on a holy day. I used to do that, so I know exactly what one should look like when standing in the proper position.

I used to be much more of a good girl than I am now....

"You want to know what the king has planned for Rose, right?" I ask him.

He nods. "Yes, of course, I do."

"All right then, my big strapping Alpha," I say as I run a hand along his arm. He looks at it, and I pull my hand away. "Here's the deal. I will gladly tell you everything you've ever wanted to know about my cousin, King Gene's, plans for the Breeder. If you...." I wiggle my eyebrows at him, hoping he gets the picture.

"If I...." He wiggles his eyebrows back at me.

"Yes, that's right," I tell him, assuming he knows what I'm getting at.

"Okay," he complies and wiggles them again. I am overjoyed that he has agreed to sleep with me until he demands, "So tell me."

My forehead puckers. "You have to do it first," I tell him.

"Yes, I know," he states firmly, wiggling his eyebrows a third time. "There, I just did it again. Tell me."

A loud sigh escapes my lips as I look at the floor and shake my head. "No, Alpha! I mean you have to...." I tip my head a bit and make a gesture with the point of my crown at the bed behind me.

"Oh." He seems confused as he mimics that movement. Is he really that dumb or is he just making fun of me?

"No! You have to fuck me!" I scream at him.

His blue eyes widen—I guess he gets it now. "No way!" he exclaims. "No way in hell I'm doing that, Emily!"

I glare at him. "Oh, you will if you know what's good for you!" I tell him. "Do you want to know what my cousin has planned for that woman of yours or not?"

His eyes twitch back and forth for a moment before he mutters, "I'll think about it."

I can't help the smile that spreads across my face. "Now, that's a good Alpha." I rest my hand on his chest, impressed by the muscle I feel beneath his shirt.

Backing up, Mark says, "Don't push it."

With a laugh, I urge him, "Come see me tonight, or the deal is off. And bring all of your toys!"

"I don't have toys," he says. "That's Tristan."

Trying not to frown that I might've picked the wrong Alpha, I reassure him, "Well, I have plenty." I wink at him. "See you later, big boy."

MARK

I walk briskly back down the hallway, thinking I need to tell the other Alphas what Emily is up to. But they will think I'm insane for even contemplating this.

Am I really thinking about sleeping with Emily in order to find out King Gene's plans for Rose?

No! I can't do it!

But maybe I can find another way….

"Think fast!" someone shouts. I turn just in time for a basketball to thump me in the side of the head. A roar of male laughter follows as I swear under my breath.

"Tristan! You asshole!" I yell.

"I told you to think fast!" he insists.

I shake my head at him. "You didn't say it fast enough." Either that, or I'm too preoccupied to think straight right now.

"We're going to go play basketball," Eli announces. "You wanna come?"

"You can tell us everything you learned about sneaky ass Emily while we play," Reece adds.

"I didn't learn anything," I tell them. It's not a lie. "Sure, I'll come." What else am I going to do?

"Great!" Tristan exclaims, bouncing the basketball on the stone floor as we walk out. "I hope your reflexes catch up to mine before we get out there."

I think they are about to be bouncing a lot of basketballs off of my cranium.

Stopping by my room, I change clothes really quickly, absently wondering where Rose went. Maybe I should've slept with her recently like the other Alphas. Maybe if I had, I wouldn't be even considering this plan of Emily's now.

It's not that I want to sleep with her. The idea puts my body in a full-on twitch. But... I do want to know what Gene has planned. Perhaps I can figure out a way to trick her into telling me.

Once I'm changed, I go outside, and without a word from anyone, I feel a ball bounce off the side of my head.

"Seriously?" I demand.

Tristan laughs. "Sorry–it was an accident."

I don't believe him, and I want to take the basketball and see if I can make his stomach look like Rose's will in a few months by shoving it up his ass, all the way through his intestines.

But instead, I just glare at him, grab the ball, and start the game. I am on Eli's team, which means I get a chance at revenge by beating Tristan.

But as we play, I'm distracted, and I keep missing shots.

What the hell am I going to do about Emily?

CHAPTER 5: NOT A GOOD IDEA

MARK

All day, I've been tortured by the idea that Emily wants to see me in her room tonight, and I don't want to go.

I know it's my best chance at getting the information we need regarding Gene's plans for Rose, but even the thought of putting a bag over Emily's head and doing her makes me sick to my stomach.

I just don't think I can do it.

Around 9:00, I get dressed in my pajamas and put on my silk bathrobe over them. I hope I don't run into anyone as I make my way down the hallway. I haven't told the other Alphas my plans at all because I didn't want to try and explain my thinking, but now, I wish I would've said something to them.

I wish I would've sought their advice....

But then... I probably would've just gotten a bunch of jokes and wisecracks, and since my head was still hurting from having gotten hit in the skull with the basketball half a dozen times earlier in the day, I really wasn't in the mood to discuss anything that might be difficult for any of them to understand.

Besides, I feel like the fewer people who know about this, the better.

As I sneak down the hallway to Emily's room, I take my time, trying to control my breathing and keep my feet light. The last thing I need is for someone to come around the corner and see me!

"Hey, Mark!"

Shit…. Like that.

I turn around and see Eli coming down a side hallway with some booze in his hands. "Hey, Eli," I greet, clearing my throat.

"Where are you off to? I was just going to get something stronger for us all to drink tonight. Well, all of us but Reece since he's with Rose right now. Where are you going?"

"Why are you asking me so many questions?" I drag my hand through my hair. "Nowhere. I'm just going for a walk."

He arches an eyebrow. "In that?"

"Yes. These are comfortable pajamas," I tell him.

Eli continues to stare at me. "Okay," he finally gives in. "Well, come join us when you get done… with your walk."

"Right," I say, and we are both eyeing each other suspiciously.

I decide I've had enough and move on, but I can feel his eyes on the back of me as I continue down the hall. I know when I turn to go down the hallway that heads toward Emily's room, he will be all over me. So I decide to go a different way… for now.

I turn toward the library and wait a few minutes before I head back down the hallway. I poke my head around the corner, and Eli is gone.

"Thank the Moon Goddess," I mutter, but as I cross the hall and head toward Emily's room, I still feel like I am being watched.

I can't think about this right now. I'm already nervous enough just thinking about what that banshee is going to say when I get to her room.

I knock on the door only once before it is flung open.

Emily is standing there, wearing some sort of leather lingerie number that leaves nothing to my imagination. It also leaves me with bile rising up in the back of my throat.

Her hair is swept back and hair sprayed in such a way that it looks like she's got wind blowing in her face.

Did I step into a music video from the 1980s?

"Hello, Marcus," she says in a deep, raspy voice, her charcoal-covered eyes stabbing through me.

"Hello?" It's a question. My name isn't Marcus. Mark isn't actually short for anything, though I used to joke that my full name was Mark Twain Gray. People don't read enough anymore to get that joke.

"Come in, Alpha," she purrs, beckoning to me with one finger.

My knees feel wobbly as I walk into her room. I feel like this is a huge mistake.

Inside of her room, I see that she's got her bed all ready to go. Gone are any signs of a normal bedspread. Instead, there are some sort of rubber sheets on the bed, and in each corner, attached to the posts, are cuffs.

"Lie down, Alpha, and I'll make sure all of your wildest fantasies come true." She attempts to smile at me, but it looks more like a snarl.

My mouth goes dry. "Uh... sure," I say with trepidation. "Maybe in a bit. I'd like to...." I look around the room, trying to figure out what we can do first. I see a bottle of wine on the table. "Have a drink first."

She sighs, rolls her eyes, and says, "Fine." She walks over to the coffee table and picks up the bottle of wine, which is mostly full but not completely. She pours two glasses and hands me one. I sit down on the couch. I want to stay as far away from the bed as possible.

She sits next to me, curling up like she's trying to get on my lap. "How was your day, gorgeous?" she asks me, running her fingers through my hair.

She smells like a flower garden puked all over her. It's not just one floral scent but about thirty-seven of them, and the flowers she's chosen don't seem to like one another. It's like they're trying to beat each other up to get away from her.

"My day was... great," I begin, realizing this is my opportunity. "I woke up at seven thirty-five. Then, I went to take a shower, but I noticed I was a little low on shampoo, so before I got into the shower, I had to go get some more, so I rummaged around under my sink, looking for some more, but I didn't have any of the same kind, which was a bummer, because I really like that shampoo. It has a nice… unassuming scent to it. Then….”

I continue to talk for at least twenty minutes while Emily refills her wine glass at least four times. I sip mine slowly. The wine has no effect on me, but I don't need to lose my head right now.

“Marcus!” she finally bellows. “Can we please just get on with it?” She goes to set the wine bottle down and misses the table. The glass bottle tumbles to the carpet, but it doesn't shatter. Nor does it spill.

I figure she has about a bottle of wine in her now. She's gotta be pretty wasted. Emily doesn't weigh that much; her boobs make up most of her mass.

“Okay,” I affirm, setting my glass down. “But I wanna tie you up.” I try to use my most alluring voice to say the words.

“No, no, no!” she refutes, wagging her finger in my face. “You get tied up, first, Marky Mark!” She bops me on the nose like I'm a puppy.

“No, no, no,” I reply back to her in a similarly annoying voice. “You first.”

Rather than getting up, she flings a leg over the top of me, so that she's straddling me on the couch. Her eyes are unfocused as she tries to speak to me. “What made you change your mind, Marky Mark?” she asks me. “Why did you decide to come and let Emily make you feel like a real man?”

I have not been expecting this question, so I'm not sure how to answer.

A lie springs to my head, and it's easy for me to tell her because it's founded in truth. “Uh, well, since Rose got pregnant, we haven't been having sex as much.” I do realize that's my fault. The other guys have continued with their turns lately. I've been the only holdout, and I feel really stupid about that now. “So I guess, I'm just having some urges.”

“Well,” she begins, her breath already turning sour from the wine, “Emily will take good care of you.” She moves her pelvis against mine, and it makes my stomach turn.

“And… Emily is going to tell me what King Gene has in store for Rose, too, right?” I remind her.

She giggles loudly. "Why? Why do you even want to know now? You've got Emily. You don't fucking need her anymore!"

"While that's true," I admit, cursing myself for even telling the lie, "I still want to know what the… miserable bitch will have coming to her." I hate myself right now for saying that about my beautiful Rose!

"Well, I will tell you everything, just as soon as you let me tie you up and whip that ass!" She tries to smile seductively at me, but she looks a lot like a drunk Jack-o-lantern that's about to tumble off of some kid's porch the day after Halloween.

Without another word, I scoop her up off my lap and carry her to the bed, still calling myself every name in the book.

What in the world was I thinking when I decided this was a good plan?

CHAPTER 6: GET DOWN ON YOUR KNEES

Emily

I've finally got one of the Alphas in my bedroom!

Now is my chance to get him to impregnate me so that I can get rid of that stupid Breeder and her four babies once and for all.

"Let me strap you down and ride you," I say to Alpha Mark as he carries me to the bed.

"No, I don't think so," he replies, dumping me onto the bed. I feel cold now, being out of his arms. I'm wearing my best leather lingerie, with bands of black that cover my nipples and my vajay-jay and little else, yet he hasn't even touched me yet.

I'm starting to wonder if Alpha Mark prefers men…. It's the only reason that he would want that manly looking Rose with the giant nose and not me.

"What do you mean you don't think so?" I ask as I try to scramble away from him.

He grabs me by the ankle and pulls me back to him. "Flip over, Emily."

His voice is deep and commanding, and it sends a shiver down my spine. "Yes, Alpha," I purr at him.

Immediately, I flip over onto my knees, assuming he wants to enter me from behind. I know he can see everything while I'm in this position, and I arch my back and relax it, spreading my legs wide so he has a great view.

Except he's not even looking at my backside. Instead, he grabs the cuffs and clips it around my left arm. Then, he moves to my left ankle and secures that. I watch as he goes around the bed to grab the cuffs on my right side and secure them into place. Now, I am cuffed to the bed.

"All right," Mark begins. "Tell me what I want to know, Emily."

I look over my shoulder at him and laugh. "Not until you do me, baby!"

"Emily, you're being very naughty," he tells me. "You tell me what King Gene intends to do to Rose, right now."

"No!" I say in my best naughty little girl voice. "I guess Daddy is gonna have to spank me!"

I see his face scrunch up and realize he's probably never role-played like this before. I continue to smile at him, gleefully.

"Fine," Mark says, another deep growl. He pulls his hand back, and a second later, my backside reverberates from his strike.

But it doesn't even hurt.

"Harder, Daddy!" I shout.

Mark hits me again in the same place. This time it smarts a little, but I want more.

"Harder, Daddy! Harder!" I scream.

He continues to smack my ass, and I moan and scream in pleasure.

"Tell me!" he demands. "Tell me right now, Emily!"

"Fine, Daddy! But then you have to fuck me!" I shout.

"I'll fuck you as soon as you tell me the truth!" Mark assures me before his hand slaps down on my big ass again.

"King Gene is going to kill that ugly motherfucker!" I shout.

The spanking stops.

"He's… what?" Mark asks.

I turn and look at him over my shoulder again. "That's right. He's going to have that fucking bitch killed the moment your babies are

THREATS AGAINST THE BREEDER

taken from her big fat stomach. And I wanna be there to watch." I smile at him, but he's not smiling back.

"Kill her?" he repeats.

I nod. "Now, fuck me like you mean it, Daddy!"

Before either of us can say more, my bedroom door flies open, and Eli comes in. "What the hell?" he asks. "Is everyone okay?"

"Oh, good. Three makes it more fun!" I cheer, looking at Alpha Eli between my knees.

"What the hell, Mark!" Eli exclaims. "I heard screaming from down the hallway and expected to come in here and see someone trying to kill Emily. I'd hoped it would be you doing that, but I can't believe what you're really doing with her. You're having sex with Emily?"

"No!" Mark shouts, but Eli turns and storms off. Mark chases after him. "Why the hell would I want to sleep with a dirty whore like Emily when I have the beautiful Rose?" I hear Mark shout.

He's gone. My bedroom door is open, and I'm cuffed to my bed... with my ass in the air.

"Mark!" I scream. "Mark! Come back here right now!"

But all I hear are footsteps echoing down the hallway in the opposite direction.

"Fuck me," I sigh and drop my face into the pillow.

MARK

I don't know how to process any of this. I can't believe that Emily has told me anything at all, but the fact that she just told me that King Gene is planning to kill Rose the moment the babies are born makes my heart sink in my chest.

I'm running after Eli, but my feet aren't traveling that fast. I stop a few feet down the hallway and slump against the wall.

"He's going to kill her?" I slouch onto the ground, my knees bent, my arms on my elbows, my head hanging low.

Rose, the most beautiful, sweetest, kind hearted, loving person in the whole world. That awful King Gene is actually planning to eliminate her as soon as the babies are born.

I can't understand it!

What would be the purpose in that? What could he possibly think of gaining by killing the mother of the next heir to the throne?

I can't answer that question. I have no idea why anyone would ever want to kill Rose. She is the most wonderful person I've ever met, and I can't think about living life without her. I can't even imagine any reality in which Rose's not in it.

But if the other Alphas and I don't find a way to stop him, King Gene will kill her. I don't think there's any chance in the world that Emily was lying.

As I drag my hand down my face, I realize it's the same hand I was just smacking Emily's ass with. I cringe and want to find a way to cut this hand off and grow a new one. Since I know I can't spawn a new hand, and I don't want to have a robot hand like some character in a sci-fi movie, I decide to leave it attached to my body and just find some really strong soap when I get back to my room.

I pull myself up off the ground and head to Eli's room where I assume he's already told Tristan and Kelly what went on. Reece is with Rose.

I'll have to find a way to convince them that what he saw was misinterpreted. Surely, they can't actually think I would stoop so low as to have sex with Emily–will they?

Making my way to the open door of Eli's room, I pause and take a few deep breaths, thinking about what I will say to explain myself.

But then I realize, what's more important than telling them why I was in Emily' room, is telling them what I discovered while I was there.

With as much oxygen in my lungs as I can suck in, I walk through the door. "Guys, I can explain."

CHAPTER 7: A CREAK IN THE NIGHT

Tristan

MARK HAS NEVER BEEN one to have a poker face, and right now it's obvious he is hiding something. Eli looks like he has just seen a cat bark. I look at both men and wonder what is going on.

"Why are the two of you chasing each other in the hallway?" Reece asks, flying through the door.

"Who is with Rose?" I ask before they can answer.

"Adam and Shelby," he assures us. "I heard a commotion."

"I will let Mark here tell us all what he was doing!" Eli announces.

We all dart our eyes toward Mark and wait for him to answer. Mark staggers a bit and still appears to be trying to catch his breath. I wonder if all the basketballs to his head messed up his coordination.

"Nothing happened. Eli, as always, is just making a mountain out of a mole hill," he finally says.

We all turn to look at Eli whose face is turning red with every word Mark utters.

"Man, are you saying I didn't just catch you red-handed snuggling with the enemy?"

I frown at this, and again we all turn to Mark. At this rate, I feel like we are all going to end up with rather painful necks.

"You saw what you wanted to see, Eli," Mark insists.

The back and forth between the two men is becoming rather unflattering suspense.

"Enough with the cliffhangers! Will one of you just tell us what the hell is going on? Why does Eli look like he's about to puke his guts up everywhere?"

This time Eli turns to face me, and a crease forms in between his eyebrows.

"Puke my guts up? Get out of here! I don't look that horrible," Eli argues.

"Do you need a mirror to confirm the comparison? Now, would someone tell us what's up? Who was snuggling with the enemy? Who is the enemy?"

Mark walks to one of the couches and slumps on it.

"Nobody was snuggling with anyone. In fact, there was no snuggling of any sort. Eli is just exaggerating," Mark confirms as he wipes his face with one hand.

"Really? Tell them where I found you, Mark. 'Ohhhh shhpank me, Marky!' Do those words ring a bell? Or do you still have amnesia?"

I can tell from Reece's face that this has piqued his interest as it has mine.

"Who were you spanking? We did hear rather loud screams. Tell us, did you beat up that witch, Emily? Oh boy, I wish you would have told us, and we could have all gone and beaten her black and blue."

"Well, there was some beating all right, but not the kind you or anyone would have wanted to join in," Mark explains.

"Argh, man. A beating is a beating. I know that I am not one to raise a hand to a woman, but if it's Emily, I can make an exception. Why would you be mad that the murderer got a beating?" I ask.

"Mark was fucking Emily. I am not sure if you would have wanted to join in that," Eli blurts out.

Eli's words make me see red, and I don't hear what anyone else is saying. My mouth feels suddenly dry, and I can feel my face getting hot like someone just left me in a sauna with all the doors closed and air vents sealed.

I stand up, hands clenched and slightly shaking, and walk toward Mark. How dare he fuck the very person who was trying to kill Rose and our children!

"So is that the reason you have been holding back from spending time with Rose? You were acting all high and mighty like everything you did was for Rose's good, yet it was just because you have been getting your fill elsewhere," I say as I move closer, wanting to punch the blank stare from his two-timing face.

"But I–" he begins but stops when the door to the room flies open and Rose walks in.

"What's going on? We heard someone screaming," she says and looks worried. Shelby is behind her, but I don't see Adam.

I stop and bring my hand to my sides trying to calm myself. I am not about to let her see me beating the daylight out of one of her baby daddies.

"Nothing, love. We are just discussing a few pack things. Nothing to worry your little pretty head about," I assure her.

She looks at me, seeming to fish out the lie with her gorgeous gaze.

"Did someone else die?"

Reece shakes his head and steps toward her. "Oh, no. No one is dead… yet."

Rose blinks at him looking confused. "What do you mean by yet?"

"The screams belonged to your baby daddy Mark and Emily," Eli bluntly states.

"Why were they screaming? Oh, my. Mark, don't tell me you beat up Emily. I know what she did was inhumane, but I thought we would let the king decide on her punishment. You didn't have to take matters into your own hands," Rose says as she walks over to where I am still standing in front of Mark, trying my best to calm down.

"I wish he had those kinds of moral intentions. He was with her… you know, with her-with her," Eli clarifies.

Rose looks over at Eli and then at Mark. Her mouth is open, but no words come out. I turn to her, and there is no denying the pain etched on her features. She is begging him to tell her this isn't true with her eyes.

"Rose, baby, you know I would ne–" Mark tries to speak but Eli cuts him off.

"Oh, yes you would. I saw you."

Rose looks like she has been slapped in the face, and my anger mounts toward Mark for hurting her emotionally. I want to take her in my arms and kiss away the confusion and pain.

"Shut up, Eli. Did you actually see me touch Emily? Tell them what you really saw," Mark growls.

"The truth is, yes. I saw you touch her ass," Eli says.

"I don't think you can intimidate Eli to support you on this one, mate. He saw you fuck Emily," Reece adds.

"He didn't see me do any such thing, and he knows it. All I was doing was playing a role to trick her into confiding her secrets to me," Mark argues.

Mark is into role-playing now too? This is all unfathomable.

"You couldn't find a better way of doing that than using your dick?" I interrogate him.

"What are you talking about? I wasn't using my dick!" Mark defends himself looking like he is about to lose it.

"Don't tell me. So you conveniently dislodged your dick and went to Emily without it? Man, you really are quite the creative mind," I say as I feign praise.

"There was no dick usage because I wasn't fucking Emily. Eli, please tell them the truth about what you witnessed."

Eli waves a hand as he walks over to sit on one of the chairs. He takes a deep breath and says, "All right, he's right. I didn't actually see him fuck her. He was fully clothed and spanking her," Eli clarifies.

We all sigh with an uneasy kind of relief.

"But wait, why were you spanking her?" I ponder aloud.

"I needed some information from the witch," Mark admits.

"So you spanked the information out of her?" I ask. Not the worst idea, I thought to myself.

"Yes, Tristan. I basically did just that. I spanked the information out of her," Mark answers.

"I am glad nothing happened, but I don't think torturing her was cool," Rose sighs. She sounds relieved to hear that nothing happened between Mark and Emily. We all know that adults spanking other adults isn't a torture method, but we all decide not to point that out to Rose.

In fact, I love a good spanking.

"Baby, I would never cheat on you. You do know that, don't you?" Mark confirms as he stands up and takes Rose's hands.

"Yeah, I guess."

"I promise, baby. I was just doing what I thought best at the time," Mark assures her and kisses her on the forehead.

She smiles and nods.

"Okay. But please, no more torturing anyone. My back hurts, and I think I should go lie down a bit. Now, the four of you play nice," she says as she smiles at all of us and walks out of the room. She leaves, and Shelby goes with her.

"So what did you find out from Emily through your spanking escapades?" Reece asks.

"Besides the fact that she has some weird fetishes and was hoping I was Tristan?" Mark says.

I glare at him, "What do you mean she hoped you were me?"

"Because she wanted me to bring my toys for us to 'play' with before she would tell me anything," Mark explains.

I feel hot bile rising in my throat.

"If Emily was to ever lay a hand on any of my toys I would burn them. Trust me, there isn't a strong enough disinfectant to get rid of whatever she would leave on them," I say, fuming.

Mark looks at his hand and frowns. "Tell me about it. Anyway, I found out what the king wants to do with Rose."

We all exchange nervous glances before I ask the question we are all waiting to have answered. "And what's that?"

Mark stares me dead in the eyes and says, "Kill her."

CHAPTER 8: ARE YOU KIDDING ME?

Tristan

"What? Why?" I ask. I had known that he was sadistic, but I don't think I was prepared for just how far the royal ass was willing to go.

"Maybe Emily was just voicing her own desires," Reece suggests, obviously also not wanting to believe that the king could be so evil.

"I believe her. King Gene has never liked Rose. Have you noticed how he never calls her by her name? He always refers to her as 'that Breeder' or 'the Breeder.' I wouldn't put this past that man," Mark says.

"Yeah, but calling her Breeder doesn't mean he wants her dead. Emily is probably lying. He wants her to give birth to the children, right? Why would he then kill her now that she's pregnant?" I wonder.

"Maybe because he knows we're all showing more personal interest in her than initially intended. He wants us to be falling for his cousin," Mark brainstorms.

"This is messed up, man. Do you think he wants to kill her before or after the children are born?" Reece asks.

"Probably after. Killing her before they're born would derail his whole plan," Eli reasons.

"His plan was to have one of us impregnate Rose. He didn't count on her getting pregnant by all of us. Either way, his plan is destroyed, so he might want to kill her before the children are born," I say. "If that was ever even his plan at all." He doesn't seem like he wants to give up the throne, in my opinion.

I walk over to the small table and take out four glasses before pouring some whiskey into each one. I'm certain we could all do with a golden alcoholic liquid pick-me-up.

"I am finding it hard to believe he'd really want her dead. Emily is a compulsive liar," I interject. Denial is the only way I can escape this unending nightmare.

"What if it's true? She was too drunk to have been lying, though," Mark says.

I take a sip from one of the glasses and invite the others to grab a glass.

"So murdering is a family thing?" I ask.

"I was wondering the same thing. Rose's life is in real danger. She'll need more protection while we try to figure out what is going on, and what the king plans to do," Eli agrees.

"Yes," I state firmly. We're all quiet for a few minutes as each of us sinks into our own thoughts. Rose has to be protected from King Gene and his cousin.

There's a knock at the door, and Eli calls out for whoever is there to come in. I find myself wondering if it was Emily eavesdropping again. I shake my head as I know that if it is her, she wouldn't be knocking to alert anyone to her rude tendencies... not that she would even understand what the word rude meant even if it hit her on the head like a boulder.

Beta Adam and his wife make their way into the room.

"Greetings, Alphas," Beta Adam says, looking unsure of why he's even in the room. He glances over at his wife, who smiles and bows slightly before smiling at her husband. It looks like she's encouraging him to say something.

"Hello, Beta Adam. It's nice of you to pay us a visit. You've never been in our common room, have you? You might know this place as

Eli's room, and I know it feels weird entering another man's space. Don't sweat it, though. Eli here is used to frequent gentlemen callers invading his space and drinking all his booze," I say, attempting a joke to make him feel at ease.

"Honestly, I do mind. But they seem set on making this their personal rendezvous area. I think it's probably because it's cleaner than their own rooms," Eli reasons and chuckles.

.

His attempt at making Beta Adam relax is definitely not as hilarious and effective as my own, but Beta Adam's shoulders lower just a bit, and I know that it has worked.

"My husband has something important to tell the four of you," Shelby, his wife, announces. She takes her husband's hand and squeezes it. I feel my mouth go dry as I wonder what's making him so nervous.

"King Gene asked me to get rid of Rose," he spits out.

Mark places the glass he is holding down on the table. I'm glad he didn't smash it this time around. "What do you mean by that?" he asks.

"After she has the children, he wants me to get rid of her."

I frown as I try to digest this. We all knew she would have to go back to her home after the birth of the children, but the way he's talking seems to imply a much sinister plot.

"Are you saying that he wants you to escort her back to her pack after she has the children?" Reece asks as his hand that is gripping the vodka glass trembles slightly. I can see his knuckles turning white from the tension. It appears today he'll be the one to smash a glass in his hand.

I walk over and rescue the glass from his grasp. The poor glasses were continuously getting the short end of the stick, not to mention the precious booze that kept on being lost in this whole process.

"He wants her killed," Beta Adam clarifies and glances down at his boots.

"We need your help. Rose's life is in danger," Shelby says and looks at the four of us with pleading, frightening eyes.

"I really thought Emily was lying. So it's true? The king wants to kill Rose?" I utter. I really want to slide my hands around the king's neck and make him wear them like shrinking jewelry.

"Do you think he's the one who sent Emily to poison Rose's food?" Mark asks.

"It could be the reason he didn't punish Emily after the fact. He must have known if he accused her she would just point the finger back at him," Reece points out.

"No, no. Emily acted on her own accord. The king wants Rose killed after she has the babies. Emily must have thought that wasn't good enough and decided to get rid of her earlier. I doubt she is too keen about raising any offspring of her nemesis," Adam explains

Mark snorts. "We also don't want her raising our children."

"What do we do?" Shelby asks, her eyes begging.

I know she hopes one of us can just wave a magic wand and make the king and his cousin disappear, but this will require strategy. I find myself wondering if we could find a sorcerer of some sort to actually make the two vanish. It would really save us from this horror.

"We'll have to go talk to the king," Mark exclaims.

"You do know you can't tie up the king and spank him into revealing his ugly side, right?" I say. Mark glares at me and bares his teeth.

"You can't go talk to him. If you do, he'll know that I told you, and that will only put us all in danger. The conversation would end up doing more harm than good," Beta Adam reminds us.

I nod as I see his point. "We have to play our cards close to the chest. Maybe we could just ask him what he intends to do since we all impregnated Rose."

"How will that stop him from killing her?" Mark asks.

"It won't stop him per se, but it will give us a reason to be talking about her. We could ask him that and then take the conversation from there," I reason.

"The father of the first male child to be born will be declared the winner," Beta Adam offers.

"What if all four children are girls?" Mark said.

Shelby crosses her arms and stares at her husband. I have been around enough women in my life to recognize an 'I told you so' stare.

"I guess we'll cross that bridge when we come to it. For now, we have to make sure Rose is kept safe, even after she gives birth," Eli says.

"We can still go by the playbook I just mentioned. For now, we'll ask him how the winner will be determined. Then, after that, one of us can suggest that the ones who don't win will escort Rose back to her home. We'll say it will be to make sure she gets there safely and doesn't get attacked by Alpha Kane or his troops," I add.

"Yeah. This will put him in a corner. If he's going to kill Rose, he won't be able to do that if she has any of us as escorts. He'll also look for an excuse if he's still going ahead with this 'killing her' plan. Then, if he finds any excuse as to why we can't escort her home, we'll grill him about why. Either way, we'll light a huge fire under his tiny ass and force him to talk," Mark says.

"Bingo! Here's to torturing people's asses to get them to sing like a canary," I say as I raise my glass.

CHAPTER 9: A RUDE WAKE-UP CALL

Kelly sits by the window, singing a tune that I recognize from my childhood. It talks about the silver moon and her flashing stars helping her look down on children. The moon guides their journey, and the stars light up their path. Kelly's red hair looks like a flame as the light from outside hits it from different angles.

"I am not a very good singer, but I will be singing the babies' lullabies when they are born. I would like them to get to know their aunt's voice now before they're born." She turns to look at me as I sit on the bed, my back propped up by some scattered cushions. "Did you know that babies can hear your voice from the womb? Their vocabulary is actually developed from there."

I smile at her as she gazes at me with starry eyes. Kelly has been reading so many baby and birthing books, one would swear she's the one carrying the babies. Since the sad poisoning of the chef, she has taken it upon herself to check on me regularly. If not for the Alphas sleeping in my room, she would have gladly had a small mattress moved in with me. I appreciate her, and her care for me and all the babies tugs at my heart like a guitarist adjusting his instrument's pitch.

"You will be the best aunt in the world," I assure her.

She jumps up from where she sits and walks toward me. "May I?" she asks, gesturing to my belly.

I nod, and she puts her ear to my belly.

"Do you feel them moving?" she asks.

"Not yet," I say. I think I glimpse a look of disappointment, but it disappears as quickly as it appeared.

"The doctor said it's just a matter of days before you start feeling their movement and kicks. Please call me the moment you feel the first kick. Whose baby do you think will throw the first punch in there?" she asks.

I giggle. "Umm, maybe Tristan's."

She joins in my little laugh. "Right? I think so too. I am sure Eli's baby will just be watching the others playing and thinking they're a bit much. Mark's baby will be warning them about causing Mommy too much pain. Reece's little one will be writing and practicing poetry inside there. Maybe you should read some poetry to them."

The prospect of the different personalities all these babies will have is endearing. I swallow and wish I would be able to watch them grow into their individual selves, but I know I'll have to give them up as soon as they're born. My heart aches at the realization that I am still going to lose my children to someone else, but I choose to swallow the bitterness of these thoughts about the future.

There's a knock on the door. Kelly grabs a golf club she put under my bed in case of danger and walks to the door.

"Who is it? If you plan to harm us, just be warned, we're armed."

I chuckle. Kelly is really protective, although I wonder if the golf club could do much to protect us.

"It's me, Eli," a voice answers from the other side of the door.

"Eli who?" Kelly asks and turns her head toward me. She winks and sticks her tongue out.

"Eli 'will knock you on the head if you don't open up.'"

"Eli 'will knock you on the head if you don't open up,' who?"

The door knob is jiggled from the other side, and since it's not locked, the door swings open.

"Huh! I didn't say come in. What if we were naked showing each other our butt cracks?"

Eli frowns at his sister. "Women show each other their butt cracks?"

Kelly nods. "Why do you think we always go to the bathroom in groups? We're showing each other our butt cracks and giving ratings and reviews."

"That's weird and disgusting. Is that true?" Eli scrunches up his face and peers at me.

I bite my lip, trying to keep myself from laughing out loud. "Uh-huh!" I nod my head.

Eli looks at me for a while before shifting his gaze to Kelly. "Women are strange."

"'Interesting' is the word you are looking for, brother."

Eli walks over and sits beside me on the bed. "How are you?" He lays a palm on my belly and smiles.

"I'm okay, and you? Did you guys sort out the whole spanking Emily saga?"

Kelly rushes toward us. "Wait! Spanking who and what?"

"Mark was trying to get Emily to tell him something, so he spanked her," I clarify.

Kelly frowns at me before turning to Eli. "Mark spanked Emily? Like, literally spanked her?"

Eli nods.

"I don't think it's a good thing to spank people," I say.

"A little spanking can be good if done properly. I'm just glad Mark gave her what she deserves," Kelly say.

I can see Eli giving his sister a stern look.

"Well, when my mother spanked me, it couldn't be labeled as good. To her, it meant I had done a bad thing," I answer.

"Yeaahhh, that's it. Spanking naughty kids. And that is exactly what Mark was doing. Spanking a very bad, bad Emily." Kelly's tone changes as she says that, which makes me raise a brow. Why was she sing-speaking?

49

"Exactly. Mark spanked a horrible girl to get information," Eli says.

"So, what information did he get from her?" I ask. I'm really curious to see if Emily was so hurt by the beating that she gave Mark the information he was looking for.

"Not much. It seemed Emily's ass is hard as a rock, just like her heart. She didn't tell him anything despite the hard spanking."

"Aww. So it was all for nothing. Did she at least confess to killing the chef?"

"Not exactly, but we already know that she did it."

I wring my hands and worry my bottom lip. "Do you think she'll try to kill me again?"

"If she tries to lay a finger on your pretty head, that will be the last thing she ever does," said Eli. "Besides, you have your own mini-army looking out for you. You have your own personal Captain Kelly Sparrow armed and dangerous with a vicious golf club right here. Honestly, though, you don't have to ever worry."

Kelly raises the golf club and mimics a striking motion. "You should see the damage I can do with a heel too."

Eli flinches when she mentions the heel, and I can't help but giggle.

"Do you want to go get some fresh air, Rose?" Eli suggests. "Remember, you still need to get those step counts in for your daily walk."

I nod. The fresh air was always magical and calming. He helps me get my shoes on and holds my hand as I get up from the bed. As we walk down the hallway, I see Mark, Reece, and Tristan coming from the opposite direction.

Mark raises his hand at me, waves, and smiles. I smile and wave back. I really miss him and wonder why he hasn't been to my room. Is he repulsed by my protruding belly and weight gain?

As we walk toward each other, I feel someone shoving roughly past me. The person pushes me so hard that I almost lose my balance. I grab at my belly protectively, praying that if I fall, I don't fall on my stomach. Eli steadies me as he curses underneath his breath. "The little witch!"

I look up to see Emily walking hastily in front of us toward the Alphas, dressed in leather underwear. Her butt is hanging out loosely from the skimpy leather material that is doing nothing to cover her up. The middle part of her leather garment is clumsily wedged in between her butt cheeks. Maybe if she was nicer, she would have friends to check out her butt crack and tell her she had a serious wedgie.

She heads toward Mark and grabs his arm. "Oh, Marky-Mark. My sugar boo. Why did you have to chase down that stupid Alpha Eli who disturbed our session? You left me hanging, daddy. I'm still wet for your lovely big cock. I'm willing to please you like you asked, since the dirty Breeder can't give you the sex you need anymore." With that, she looks back over her shoulder at me with snake-like eyes.

So, my suspicions were true? Mark hadn't come to be with me because he was repulsed by me? Now he was choosing Emily over me. He had used and discarded me like a piece of tissue. How could I have been so stupid?

I feel a stabbing pain in my chest. My vision is blurry, and it isn't because of the tears. My legs feel like jelly under me, and I can feel them giving out from under me. Suddenly, everything turns white, and I slump into nothingness.

CHAPTER 10: ROSE FIRST AND FOREVER

Mark

"What the fuck, you wh–" I start saying to the annoying female shifter form in front of me, but then I catch a glimpse of Rose slipping to the floor.

Eli is fast enough to catch her before she hits the ground. I shove Emily to the side, and she falls to the floor with a little scream. I know I didn't push her that hard, and this is all her overacting. I actually wish I had put my back into shoving her.

"Oh, Marky. I think I hurt my ankle," she cries after me as I rush toward Rose.

The other Alphas are right behind me. We all crouch beside her as she lies in Eli's arms.

"Is she okay?" I ask Eli.

He raises his eyes to me. They seem to be shooting invisible arrows into my face. "Does she look okay?" he utters.

This is all my fault. I wanted to get information from Emily, but maybe there was a better way to do that.

"Did she hear what Emily said?" I ask.

"She's pregnant, not deaf, bro," Tristan spits sarcastically.

I run my fingers through my hair and just want to collapse beside

53

her. I put the back of my hand in front of her nose. "She's breathing," I say, relieved.

"Yeah, I'll carry her back to her room," Eli offers and starts to lift her up.

"Please let me do that. I want to be with her," I offer as I grab Eli's arm.

Eli shifts Rose's weight into my arms. I gently lift her, cradling her to my chest before standing up.

"Lift with your legs," Tristan demands.

"Fuck off!" I growl at him.

He smirks but grabs my arm as I start to walk away. "Take care of her, bro. Make things all right, please."

I nod and proceed toward Rose's room.

"So none of you are going to carry me to my room?" I hear Emily ask as I walk away.

When I get into Rose's room, I gently place her on the bed and cover her with a blanket. I take a chair and sit beside the bed, watching her. Stroking her hair, I stare at her gorgeous face. I love how radiant her face is looking due to the pregnancy.

"You are gorgeous," I say, but I wonder if she can hear me. I inch my face closer to hers and kiss her forehead. "I love you."

She stirs just a little, and my heart leaps as I wait for her eyes to open, but they don't.

"The first time I saw you, my one question was, 'Who is that girl?' I've met lots of girls in my life, but something special about you drew me in. When I found out that you were the one who'd be carrying our children, I was overjoyed.

"When we raced in our wolf forms to have you first, I ran as though my life depended on it. It did, really, because I wanted to be with you your first time. Not just because you were a virgin, but because I wanted to personally make sure your first night would always be memorable, not some duty you were forced into, but an action to transform you into a woman. My woman. My life."

I take a deep, shaky breath and look around the room. I find talking to myself a bit awkward, but this is the best time to pour out all these feelings I've kept bottled inside of me.

"Do you believe in love at first sight, baby? Well, I think I loved you from the very first moment I laid my eyes on you. From then on, I knew there could never be anyone else. I didn't sleep with Emily, and I don't want her. I only want you, now more than ever. I've just been afraid of hurting you or the babies; that's why I stayed away. I knew that if I got close to you, I wouldn't be able to keep myself from touching you. I also couldn't admit to anyone that I, Alpha Mark, am afraid. I'm not good at displaying my weaknesses."

Clear liquid trickles down my cheek, catching me off-guard. I swipe at it and chuckle.

"Speaking of a weak-ass man, look at this. I've never cried for a woman, you know? I just love you so fucking much it hurts and scares me. I would never want to hurt you. If I do, please know that wouldn't be my intention. Emily had intel that I needed, and since she wouldn't give me the intel she had, I played a role. The role only involved me spanking her, but that's where it ended."

I lean on her arm and allow the tears to flow freely. "Please be okay, baby. I'm sorry. I'm such an idiot and a fool, a fool in love with you."

I feel more tears hitting the bedding underneath Rose's arm.

"I'm glad you can't see me crying. Who knew Alphas cry?" I whimper as I nestle my nose under her arm.

"Actually, I love a man who isn't afraid to show his true emotions."

I raise my head and see Rose looking at me as I lay my head beside her arm. I swipe away at my tears with urgency. I open my mouth to laugh, but what comes out is a mixture between a groan, yelp, and hoarse chuckle.

"I'm so glad you're awake," I exclaim with a voice so sharp I don't even recognize it as my own. "I was just about to call the healer."

"I'm okay, and I've been awake for most of your speech." She smiles with a mischievous grin.

I run my palm over my face. "You heard all that?"

"Uh-huh!"

I feel my face warm. "I'm sorry about all the emotion."

"Why are you sorry? I loved every word. And you actually look more handsome when you cry."

"Oh, now I know that's not true," I say as I feel my face's core temperature spike.

"Oh, yes you are. You really didn't sleep with Emily?"

"I swear on my ugly tear-stained face I didn't. I would never do that to you."

"So you just spanked her? For some information of sorts?"

I nod, feeling guilty about even that. I should have looked for another way to gather my information. I am such a fool.

"Promise me that you'll never compromise your integrity again," she demands, her eyes searching mine.

"I promise," I assure her.

She looks over my shoulder to an empty corner of the room. "Are you repulsed by me?"

I jerk my head back. "What? Why would you ever think that?"

Rose bites her lip and looks back into my eyes. "Why, then, have you refused to come to see me and spend time with me since I became pregnant?"

"Because I'm an idiot. I want you now more than ever. I was just scared, baby. I don't want to hurt you or the babies." Maybe she hadn't heard that part of my speech, or maybe she needed to hear it again to believe it.

She smiles at me and inclines her head to the side, blinking and licking her lips; the action makes my dick twitch in my pants.

"I want you, Mark. You've been keeping me waiting for too long. Make love to me," she says as if it was a direct command. "I want you to touch me again and ravish me, just like you did the first night we spent together."

I don't need more coaxing. I've missed her so bad. I stand up and take off my clothes. When I remove my pants, my manhood springs forward in her direction. It's as though it knows where it belongs and is pulling me to her. Her eyes move to gaze at it, and she licks her lips.

"Stop doing that. I'll come undone just by your stare."

She giggles and sticks a pinky in her mouth. I step forward.

"Touch me, baby," I say.

She obliges, and I quickly realize this was a bad move considering it's been so long. Her warm touch makes the blood rush to my head, causing sparks to flash in my vision.

I get on the bed and lay beside her. She shifts her body to give me enough space. I balance my weight on one arm and bend down to kiss her neck. She pushes her chin up, exposing raw flesh. I nibble and suck at it, and I'm rewarded with a moan.

When I raise my head, she has a bright red mark on her neck. I smile at the hickey that seems to be darkening by the minute.

I run my hand from her shoulder down her body, pushing away the flimsy material that is keeping me from feeling and touching her skin. As my hand reaches her breasts. I gasp at how much fuller they feel. She has quickly turned from the shy girl I first lay with to this voluptuous woman lying next to me on the bed.

I lightly squeeze the mound of flesh and flick her nipple softly with my thumb. She gasps as

I move down until I am touching lace and I trace the hem of her panties and push them to the side. She grinds against me, and I groan, the sensation causing me to inch forward, wanting more.

Removing her panties completely, I ease myself inside her warm core. Her muscles envelope and welcome me. They tighten around my rod and encircle it with moist bliss. I rock forward, and she whines, her hips meeting my every thrust with such intensity that I'm fighting to hold on to my sanity.

Moving back ever-so-slightly, I allow the tip of my cock to circle the entrance of her core, probing, teasing. She inclines her head back, her moans begging for me to take her again.

I inch back forward, and she moves her hips to meet my hungry plunge, taking me all in at once. I feel her muscles tighten around me again. Her screams further assure me of her release.

I can feel her sweet walls vibrate against my hard flesh, and I let go, completely coming undone on top of her trembling body.

CHAPTER 11: THE ANSWER

MARK

When the first light of the day shines through the lace curtains in Rose's room, she is still asleep, leaning her head on my chest. I know I have to go meet with the other Alphas, but I really don't want to leave her. I let them know the night before that she is fine using the mind-link.

I kiss the top of her head, and her eyes flutter open.

"Morning, love," I whisper groggily, praying I don't have morning breath.

She rubs her face onto my chest, and I wonder if maybe I do, in fact, have morning breath.

"Morning," she answers.

"Kelly will be up shortly with your breakfast," I tell her.

She smiles and yawns, making a cute sound. "I guess you have to leave now?"

I nod. She tries to sit up, and I help her.

"I'll come and check on you later, baby."

When I finally leave, she's in the bathroom, freshening up for the day. I fight every urge to join her in the shower.

Going to my room, I manage to have a quick shower and brush my teeth before heading over to Eli's room. The other Alphas are already there when I arrive.

"Hey, look who's here," Eli says as I enter the room. The smell of toast, bacon, and eggs greets me when I enter, making my mouth water.

"Since when do we have breakfast in here?" I ask, confused.

"Since y'all decided you love my room so much you turned it into your personal man cave," Eli replies humorlessly.

I walk over to the table where an assortment of food, coffee, and juice is laid out. I start buttering a slice of toast and then pour myself some orange juice.

"So I heard someone weeping last night in Rose's room. The voice didn't sound feminine, it sounded rather deep... like this," Tristan says as he proceeds to bray, mimicking a donkey.

"Shut up!" I yell.

"Ohhh, boy. What was she doing to you that made you cry like that?" Tristan asks.

"Nothing I want to discuss with any of you," I answer, and I bite into my toast.

"Maybe she was getting her revenge. He spanked Emily, so maybe she was spanking him," Reece says and snickers.

I give him a stern sideways glance.

"Whatever she did, man, she really had you going. It's okay though. We know it's been a while since you got some. The release of all that tension must have been explosive," Eli exclaims.

I want to tell him he doesn't know the half of it, but I'm not one to kiss and tell.

"So, when are we going to go talk to the king?" I ask.

"We already did," Tristan tells me. My eyes bulge at him.

"Really? Without me?"

Eli nods. "We couldn't wait. He told us that he has no intentions of hurting Rose," Eli says.

"Well, he's a lying ass-head, so we have to be careful. Of course, he assured us that 'the Breeder' will be kept safe after giving birth and returned to her home. He wouldn't be stupid enough to admit that he wants to get rid of her," I warn.

"You know who we need to get rid of?" Reece asks.

"The lying ass-head?" Tristan asks.

"Emily," Eli clarifies.

"You should have allowed me to spank her that night, Marky-Mark. I would've spanked her right into another dimension. Problem solved. Spanking is not for the softies; it's for seasoned experts like myself," Tristan exalts himself, making us all laugh.

"I think if you ask her nicely, she might just allow you to spank her. I don't think she was satisfied with Marky-Mark," Reece adds.

"Argh, nah. I have a better plan. I can dip my magic wand sex toy into the water so when she rubs her privates with it, she gets electrocuted. Bye-bye little piggy," Tristan cackles maniacally.

We all turn and gape at him.

"Why in the world do you have a magic wand sex toy?" Reece asks. "And why would it work that way?"

"'Magic' is the key word bro." Tristan wiggles his eyebrows at him and licks his lips. "The ladies love that shit. Sex and magic, I do that well."

I pick up some bacon and shove it in my mouth. Last night Rose and I made love twice, and I feel like I need to replenish my energy.

"Should we ask the kitchen to send up more food, Marky-Mark?" Tristan asks.

"Stop calling me that," I growl at him.

"Why, Marky-Mark? The name suits you. Did Rose transfer some of her pregnancy hormones to you during the rhumba in between the sheets? You're shoving in food like you're eating for five," Tristan continues.

"Allow the man to eat. We need solutions, and Marky-Mark thinks better when he is well fed," Reece says patronizingly.

"Stop calling me that," I warn him.

"Yes, guys. Come on. Stop calling Marky-Mark that," Eli declares.

I take a sip of my juice and roll my eyes. Fighting this name is only urging them on.

"I think the only way to get rid of Emily is to find her another suitor," I suggest.

"See, I told you he thinks better on a full tummy. Just a few quick questions. Where will we find this suitor? How will we get Emily to fall for him? Will the king let her marry someone else?" Reece asks reasonable questions.

I take another sip of my juice.

"Yes, drink that magic juice. We need your awesome brain to think," Tristan cheers.

"We'll invite some Alphas and Betas to the palace for her. Their job is the easiest part; Emily will fall for anyone who's willing to play her games. A little spanking here, a little feather tickle there, a few charming words thrown into the mixture, and bam! Wedding bells," I explain.

"Are you sure this will work?" Eli asks.

"All that girl needs is a bunch of men showering her with attention, fighting over her, even. The moment she feels like she is now the belle of the ball, she'll focus her energy there," I reason.

"I think that could work. What about King Gene? Will he let her be with someone else?" Tristan asks.

"He has a soft spot for his cousin. She also has a way of making him do whatever she wants. If she bats her eyelashes at him and tells him she's in love, he'll let her go," I predict.

"We should give all of this a try then. I just hope it works," Tristan says.

I finish up my juice. "It has to," I say defiantly.

"Any ideas on the list of Alphas and Betas we should invite?" Eli asks.

"We should sit down and come up with a great list. We'll ask Beta Adam to help organize all of this," Reece coordinates.

I pour myself another glass of juice, wondering why the other guys haven't touched the food. "Why are you guys not eating?" I ask.

"You're eating enough for all of us," Reece teases.

"If this food is poisoned, that means I'll be the only one who dies," I point out.

"The food isn't poisoned. In the early days, I might have considered getting rid of the three of you so I'd have Rose all to myself. But now I feel like we are the Musketeers," Tristan says.

"Musketeers?" I look at him confused.

"Yeah. You know that reference. From The Three Musketeers? Don't tell me you never read that book as a child," Reece raises an eyebrow at me. "Although, there are four of us instead of three."

I try to think if I remember anything of that sort, but nothing comes to mind. "Nope, I don't know the book," I answer.

"Okay, we are the Galaxy Defenders team. And when we combine our forces, we become Voltron," Tristan says. "Maybe you watched cartoons?"

"Who's Voltron?" I ask. I suddenly feel like I've been living under a rock.

Tristan shakes his head with a look of disappointment on his face. "Never mind. We've all eaten already, so if the food was poisoned, we'd all be dead. Also, all my references mean that we make a great team, and I wouldn't share this experience with anyone else but the three of you."

We all nod in agreement, glad someone has finally said it.

CHAPTER 12: THE FOOL GETS FOOLED

"Do you think the Alphas know about our plan to get rid of the Breeder?" King Gene asks as he paces up and down behind his huge executive desk. I feel like I have to strain my neck to see him properly as the height of the desk dwarfs his small stature even more.

"No," I lie. My heart is racing, but I take the calming breaths that Shelby taught me whenever she insists I join her in her yoga routines.

"They were here and asked me what would happen to her after she gave birth. I could have sworn they knew something," he says.

I inhale and count slowly to five. I exhale sharply and then answer, "They have no idea. I'm sure they're just concerned about her safety as a result of Alpha Kane's threats and also because of the unfortunate death of the chef. All these events are enough to rattle anyone. I'm sure they have no clue about your plans to get rid of the Breeder."

It hurts me to refer to Rose as 'the Breeder.' It sounds so animalistic, so belittling.

He stops pacing and peers at me from behind the desk. I wonder if he's standing on his tippy toes just to try to get a better view of me. I pray my face doesn't betray anything. I try to fill my mind with images of Shelby's naked body so he can't see the fear in my eyes.

"All right. That's fine. Just continue to keep this plan between us. Not even your wife can know about this. You don't want her thinking of you as a helpless woman murderer," he threatens.

I bite my inner lip. How dare he try to use my wife as a guilt trip? I'm not a murderer; he is.

"Yes, Your Majesty," I answer and bow slightly.

He waves me away, and I leave the room.

I rush down the hallway, wanting nothing but to confide in my wife. I know she'll make me feel better. She is my personal cheer-leader, and I need to be with her now.

Shelby jumps when I burst into the room. I can tell she wasn't expecting me. "You scared me," she says as she clasps her chest.

"I'm sorry, love. I just needed to come and be with you. King Gene was asking me if the Alphas found out about his plans," I tell her.

Shelby smiles at me. She is wearing a chiffon top and jeans, and I can see the outline of her bra underneath her blouse. "So, what did you tell him?"

"I told him they have no idea. Was I supposed to tell the truth?" I ask.

"Of course not, my love. I know you threw the idiot off the scent with ease. There's a good reason you are the Beta, my smart man. I'm so proud of how you are handling all this, my loving man. You are fighting for the innocent, and this is just making you even more attractive to me," she admits and steps toward me.

Shelby stands in front of me and kisses me on the lips, her free hand going to the bulge in my jeans. My hands slowly massage her back, before moving one hand down to her ass–the other returning to her lovely breasts.

She skillfully unzips my fly and works her hand into my shorts, pulling out my throbbing manhood. She slowly starts caressing it, never breaking our kiss as I moan at the sensation of her hand engulfing my hard cock.

She breaks the kiss and steps back. I watch her pull her top over her head, and then she quickly unclasps her bra. I gulp as I take in her hypnotizing beauty, enhanced by the light filtering into the room from outside.

Her breasts are perfect. Her gratifyingly perky nipples somehow magically invite me to suck on and play with them. I stare into her eyes. She gazes at me hungrily and leans forward to reclaim my lips, kissing and caressing. Her hand returns to give attention to my hard dick.

I transfer my kisses from her lips to her neck as she works to undo my pants. She gasps as I take one breast in my hand, and then I alternate between both of her nipples and begin to suck hard on them. My jeans slide to the ground and her hands move to my ass and grasps it, her nails digging deep into my flesh.

My hands move slowly but lovingly down her body, sliding around her waist. I move to the front and begin to undo the top button of her jeans–her hands grab mine and she whispers huskily, "Not yet, darling."

She sucks, blows, and heavily breathes in my ear. I utter a growl. I can tell she wants to tease me, but being forced to wait for the immense pleasure of entering her is both frustrating and exciting. I want to scream.

She pulls me toward the bed, kissing me before pushing me onto the mattress. She helps me take off my shirt and begins to trail kisses down my chest as my fingers stroke her cheek and grab at her hair.

Her hands grab my hardness, sliding down around my balls as well. I think I stop breathing for some time, holding my breath in anticipation as she kneels and gently blows on my sensitive flesh.

Shelby chuckles as I squirm, and then I feel the hotness of her breath consume my manhood and feel the pressure as she sucks on the tip, her tongue flicking with such skill and precision. Her hand begins to gently slide up and down my rod.

She strokes my manhood a few times and then the warmth of her mouth engulfs me again. Her tongue and fingers work expertly as her lips slide up and down. My hands go into her hair. I gently pull her down as she drives me quickly near the edge. I whisper her name, but as I do, she stops. My world is spinning.

I begin to slide my hands down to undo her jeans again. She slaps playfully at my hands and flashes me a smile. She kisses me lightly again and then stands up. I watch as she slides out of her jeans, very slowly.

When her jeans are off, she straddles my hips. I can feel the fabric of her panties and the heat of her pussy encompass my manhood. My hands slide up her legs, but she swats them away again, grinding hard against my cock. I can feel the wetness of her on me and I ache to be inside her. I close my eyes. "Shelby...."

I feel her warm body on my chest as she kisses me again. She sits up and grabs my dick with one hand and slides her panties to the side with the other as she guides me inside of her.

We both moan with the sensation, and I can feel her convulse as I fill her. She slowly rocks her hips, and I keep my hands firmly on her waist, guiding her speed.

Shelby throws her head back and moans with every stroke. We are both lost in the sensation, her speed picking up a bit as she arches her back. I slide my hand up and begin rubbing her most sensitive nub with my thumb. She lets out a quiet moan of pleasure, and her nails dig into my chest. She keeps going; riding me, losing herself as I pound into her again and again until finally, she throws her head back and screams.

I feel her whole body shudder as she reaches the peak of her release. Her muscles grip me as we continue to build a perfect rhythm. I groan and allow myself to reach my own release. A moment later, she collapses on top of me, and we kiss passionately again.

Shelby lays beside me as we both reminisce in the post-passion euphoria.

A few moments later, I'm able to speak again. "Alpha Reece told me of a plan they have to invite suitors to the palace for Emily. I'm in charge of inviting some Alphas and Betas to try to capture her interest. We hope she falls for one of them. That way, we'll be rid of the Emily problem," I explain.

Shelby snuggles closer to me. "Don't invite Alphas. Just invite Betas. That way she gets to marry a Beta and not an Alpha."

I frown down at her. "What's wrong with marrying a Beta?"

"Nothing, my love. Just a Beta is well suited to take care of that sexually starved minx. If she has a taste of what I get, she won't give the Alphas a second thought," she says.

I feel my face warm up and my heartbeat quickens. "Really?"

"Of course," she answers.

I roll her over onto her back and kiss my way down her body, taking in her neck, her nipples, her belly, her thighs, and the entire length of her body. I kiss my way up her legs, nibbling and teasing the inside of her thighs as she squirms in anticipation. I'm ready to go again.

CHAPTER 13: KNOWLEDGE IS POWER

Rose

Something is bothering my men, but they don't want to talk about it. Instead, they talk about silly things. They don't even want to talk about the babies because they know how I feel about the fact that they won't be mine for long.

They also want me to stay in my room as much as possible, which is getting very boring. I would rather at least go out and walk in the garden or explore a bit in the forest, but they tend to think that, with Emily on the prowl, it's best if I just stay inside.

I'm feeling so bored, I am practically swinging from the rafters.

Eli is in the room with me. It's his turn to babysit. He's sitting in the chair across from mine by the window, and we are both allegedly reading. He does look like he's caught up in the book he's holding. From the cover, it looks like he's reading a story about wolf shifters who hunt down other mythical creatures, like vampires and fairies.

I scoff. As if vampires and fairies really exist!

"What?" Eli asks, ripping his eyes away from the book.

"Nothing," I dismiss with a shrug. I balance my romance book on the armrest next to me. "I was just thinking that your book looks really silly, that's all," I tell him with an air of nonchalance. I brush my hair back over my shoulder and begin to fidget with a loose thread from the chair.

I'm bored out of my mind!

"Silly?" Eli asks, an amused, yet offended, look taking over his handsome face. "I beg your pardon, dearest, but my book is anything but silly."

"Vampires?' I ask him. 'Fairies? Like those even exist…." I shake my head at him, and a small grin pulls up at the corner of his mouth.

"Hey, you never know," he says, dog-earing the page he's on and setting the book aside.

"Some people would call you a barbarian for treating a book that way," I mutter.

"Are you one of those people?" he asks. "Because you're the only one here, and the only one that matters."

"No," I defend. "I don't care what you do to that stupid book. It's silly anyway." I'm baiting him, and I think he knows it. I'm just so tired of sitting around, reading, eating, and occasionally having sex with one of my four men.

Okay, I'm not tired of that, but I really need more to do than just those few things.

Besides, Eli has been acting standoffish today, and I think he's just trying to make it seem like we have more to do than have sex.

But right now… I can't think of much else to do.

"What about your book?" he asks me, eyeing my novel. "That looks kind of silly, too. Why does that dude on the front cover have his shirt open, blowing in the wind? Does he shave his chest to make it look so smooth?"

I pick up my book and look at the cover, holding it open so I don't lose my page.

The man on the cover is wearing a long blue military jacket with red trim and yellow trousers. The woman has on an elaborate gown and is leaning her head against his bare chest, her own gown falling down around her lower arms, her breasts spilling out the top like a melon cart that's been tipped on its side.

"I mean… they are on the beach," I remind him. "It is probably warm out there. I can't really remember what it's like to go outside, but I think sometimes it gets hot out there, doesn't it?" I look out the window as if that might jog my memory of the sensation of being out of this room.

He rolls his eyes at me. "We let you go outside sometimes," he declares.

"Not for days," I tell him. A blue bird flutters by my window, and I listen to its pretty song for a moment before it flutters away. It must be nice to be so free and be able to leave whenever one wants....

"It's not safe, Rose," he says, his voice low, and I nod my head. I know he's right. Eli clears his throat, and I turn to look at him. "Does that book have any... suggestions?"

"Suggestions?" I repeat, my eyebrows raising. "Suggestions for what?"

"For... things we could try," he says with a shrug.

I thumb through the page as I think about what I've read so far. "Well, we don't have a beach in the castle, so I guess we can't try that," I tell him. "And I'm pretty sure we don't have a pirate ship." I sigh.

"We could see if we could make the bed rock like a boat on the water," he suggests.

"What do you mean? Invite someone in to shake it back and forth while we make love on it? I don't think I need an audience."

He laughs at my joke. "No, not that...."

"Well, I don't know what else we can do," I say, setting the book aside. I glance at the page number before I close it, hoping I can remember it later.

"What about... that other thing, the thing... Mark and Emily were allegedly doing?" he asks me, and my eyebrows arch immediately.

"You wanna spank me?" I ask him.

"No!" Eli says quickly. "Not that!"

"You want me to spank you?" I consider it. Maybe I should smack his ass a few times.

He laughs. "Absolutely not! No, I meant, when I walked into the room, Emily was tied up. Maybe I could tie you up?" he asks in his normal voice, not a sultry bedroom one, and it almost sounds as if he'd like to kidnap me if I'm willing.

I have done things like that with Tristan, but it seems a little strange to go there with Eli when he is so sweet and gentle compared to Tristan.

I'm so bored, I'm willing to try just about anything.

"Okay." I agree to his proposal.

His eyes widen in disbelief. "Okay?"

"Sure," I say. "But I don't have any handcuffs."

"That's okay. I'll use… something else." He looks around the room like he might find something that will substitute for handcuffs.

Seeing nothing, he goes to my drawer and pulls out a pair of pantyhose. "This will work," he says.

I shake my head at him as he tosses them on the bed, and then, with a wide grin on his face, he flings himself at me and starts kissing me.

He is not sweet and gentle this time as he kisses me hard and begins to tear at my clothes like I'm wearing gift wrap. We are both undressed in record time, and he motions for me to get up on the bed, which I do.

Then, Eli wraps the hose around my wrists, binding them together before he ties them to the spokes of the headboard.

"How does that feel?" he asks me.

"Like my wrists will be joining the eighty-year-old women in the temple for worship service on Sunday?" I say with an air of sarcasm.

He makes a face at me. "What?"

I shrug. Does anyone wear pantyhose anymore? I don't know anyone that does. I don't even know why I have these.

"I think we need a blindfold," he announces.

"Well, unless I also have some black stockings, I don't think you're going to find anything that can reach all the way around my head."

"A sock?" he asks me.

"All I have are anklet socks," I reply.

"What about mine? I have tube socks," he proposes, looking over his shoulder at the floor.

"Uh, if you're thinking of wrapping a dirty sock around my face, I'll go ahead and pass. Just get on with it, Eli," I tell him. "I'll just close my eyes."

"But I want you to enjoy this," he says in a bit of a whiney voice.

"I will. Just do it already!" We sound like we've been married for twenty years.

At my insistence, he presses inside of me, and I can tell our discussion has made him a little softer than usual, but the more he thrusts, the harder his cock becomes, and then he's kissing me and sucking on my tits, which feels different with my arms tied up above my head. I lift my hips and buck against him.

This is not a graceful, enticing dance, but it gets the job done, and within a few moments, I am shrieking in pleasure, cheering him on, swearing at him, encouraging him to fuck me harder. It feels kind of good to have this sort of release when I've been pent up in the room for so long.

When he finally quickens his pace and tightens up and then shoots into me, I feel like I've run a few miles. I'm sweaty, out of breath, and a little sore.

Eli is panting as he collapses next to me. He lays there for a few minutes before his breathing evens out, and I realize... he's fallen asleep.

"Eli?" I say in a whisper at first. I am still tied to the bed, after all. He says nothing.

"Eli?" I'm a bit louder this time.

He starts to snore, and I growl at him in annoyance.

"Eli!" I scream.

He opens his eyes. "Huh?"

"Untie me!" I insist.

He laughs and says, "Right," before he reaches up and unbinds my hands. I give him a playful shove, and he grabs me, pulling me against his chest.

I snuggle against him, and we fall asleep in each other's arms.

CHAPTER 14: THAT MAGICAL WAND

ROSE

"So... Eli tells me you're bored," Tristan says as he walks into my room the next day to take over his shift. He is carrying a large black bag, one I've seen before, the one he carries his toys in.

I can't help but grin at him. "Well, I have been locked up in my room for a while now."

"Yes, locked up in your room and also held hostage by old lady underwear," he jokes as if Eli has told him everything.

A laugh bursts through my lips. "That's true," I admit. "I don't even know why those were in my drawer."

"I don't know. Maybe an old woman used to sleep in this room." It is a possibility, I suppose. I hope that the old woman who used to own those pantyhose didn't actually wear them.

She'd better hope she never has to wear them again.

"Well, I have plenty of toys to keep us busy," Tristan assures me. "And real handcuffs, too. None of that makeshift elderly person drawers business." He pulls out some cuffs that look long enough to reach from the center of the bed to each of the posts, and there are four of them. They're black velvet cuffs with black chains, and they are much more of a turn on than the pantyhose Eli found.

But in fairness, the pantyhose had done their job.

"Now, take your clothes off, little flower," Tristan demands. "Take them off really slowly. I want to savor every moment of you stripping."

He is demanding, and I like that. I stand and take a few steps closer to him. He had been standing in the middle of the room, but now, he pulls out a chair from the dining room area and sits in it.

I do as he asked, taking my time, peeling every layer of clothing off slowly and watching his eyes as he gasps with wonder, as if he's never seen my body before.

At one point, I think maybe he hasn't when he gasps, "You've got a baby bump!"

"I know," I assure him, my hands nestling beneath my protruding abdomen. "I'm pregnant, Tristan."

He laughs at me and shakes his head slightly. "I hadn't noticed it before."

I can't believe he hasn't noticed because I feel like I've looked as if I swallowed a whole watermelon for months, but he's right, I haven't been showing this much for long. "Well, these are the children," I tell him.

He stands then, and I am down to my thong, so I've almost done everything he wanted. He rubs my belly and then drops down to his knees and kisses a line across where the babies are nestled together softly in my tummy.

When he's done, he stands, and his demeanor changes. "Drop your thong."

"Yes, sir," I declare, a shiver tingling down my spine.

I drop my thong, and he leads me over to the bed, where he takes his time securing all four of my limbs to the bed. "You comfortable?" he asks me.

"Yes, as long as you don't forget about me," I reply.

"Huh?"

He knows there's something there, but I don't want to sell Eli out by telling Tristan he fell asleep with me still tied up. "Nothing."

Tristan strips down to his underwear, tight red briefs that show me he's already hard for me. He pulls a black blindfold out of the bag and secures it around my face, and I almost immediately start laughing.

"What is it?" he asks me.

"Nothing," I assure him but then can't help but add, "but it doesn't smell like the gym."

"It had better not," he says. The bed shifts as he bounds back off it, and then, I have to surrender my sense of sight and rely on everything else, namely feel.

Something soft brushes against my skin, from my stomach up to the valley between my breasts. It feels like a feather, but I know he doesn't like for me to ask questions while he's playing with his toys, so I remain silent and try to concentrate on how good it feels. He runs the feathered object all over me. Then, he switches to something a little rougher, but it still feels good.

Next, I hear a strange vibrating noise, and I immediately think of the toy I have in my drawer.

But this is louder. The purr reminds me of the roar of a boat engine.

I am a little frightened, so I ask, "What is that?"

"This..." he begins, "is my magic wand. I don't use this with just anyone, and I don't use it very often."

"I sure hope you cleaned it since the last time you used it," I mumble.

"Of course! I would never use unsanitized toys, Rose," he replies.

"It sounds big," I say with a cautious tone.

"It is. It's huge," Tristan exclaims. For a moment, I think I should clarify that I'm talking about the toy, not his dick. "But I won't insert it inside of you this time, little flower. It might take out one of the babies, or at the very least, make them blind in one eye."

"Well, don't maim the children!" I advise him.

He only laughs.

Then, I feel the object he has been holding on my thigh, and I am no longer in a humorous mood. It is huge, and the end of it is vibrating so quickly, it sends a thrill of electricity shooting through my body.

He runs it up one thigh and down the other, and I find myself bucking, wishing he'd run it against my folds.

But instead of doing that, he lifts it and places it against my left nipple, and I bite into my bottom lip and moan as he runs it across my chest to my other nipple.

"You like that?" Tristan asks in a husky voice.

"Yes," is all I can manage to eke out as I'm feeling breathless.

"Good," he affirms. "Your nipples are so hard.

I feel his breath on me before he takes my left nipple into his mouth and sucks on it, hard, his wand on my other nipple. I can't even tell which one feels better, but I want to press his head further against me. I can't move, though, which makes it even more enticing.

Tristan draws his head away, and then, he lowers his magic wand, and the vibrating hits my outer folds. I gasp and lift up slightly, my body wishing he would move it inside. He doesn't, not yet, and I am practically begging him to with my body language.

Tristan is amused, but when he uses his hand to open me wide, holding my most sensitive spot between his fingers, I am already on fire.

Then, he presses the magic wand against me, and I am set aflame. I buck my hips and arch my back, moaning and crying out as my mind goes fuzzy from all of the pleasure his toy is bringing me.

"Feels good, doesn't it, little flower?" he asks me.

"Goddess… yes," I manage to hiss out. I fall over the edge within a matter of seconds, and my mind goes fuzzy from wave after wave of desire.

I want to beg him for more and also push him away, but without being able to use my hands, and unable to speak because I can't breathe, I am at Tristan's mercy.

He can read my body perfectly, though, and when he knows I can't take anymore, he pulls it away, and then I feel the bed adjust again as he's off and then back onto the mattress.

When he pushes inside of me, I am already so sensitive, I cry out immediately. He fills me and stretches me beyond my capabilities, and he is pounding into me hard. It feels so good, but every time he touches my clit, I feel like I'm going to split in two.

Tristan doesn't take his time, which I appreciate, because I am spent. He jerks a few times and empties his seed inside of me, and I feel one last flicker of lightning shoot through me.

Then, he collapses onto the mattress next to me, struggling to catch his breath.

I focus on bringing air into my lungs, but when I'm finally able to breathe again, a wave of panic washes over me as I say, "Tristan? Don't forget to–"

"On it, little flower," he assures me, and I feel his fingers brushing against my wrists as he uncuffs me.

I breathe a sigh of relief. I was a little concerned he might leave me that way, but soon enough, I'm free. He removes the blindfold and crushes me to his chest. He kisses me, and I kiss him back, exhausted.

I want to see his magic wand just so I know what he was using to make my body feel so good, but I don't dare ask because, knowing Tristan, if I ask to see his magic wand, it won't be the toy he shows me, and he'll think I'm ready for round two.

And I'm gonna need more time to recover from that!

CHAPTER 15: HERO ON THE SCENE

Rose

Having sex with my men is always fun, but in between, I feel bored, and the fact that the babies are starting to get bigger means that I am getting bigger, too.

I wonder how long it will take for me to be so big that sex is no longer comfortable at all.

It probably won't be long now, I think as I stare into the mirror and rub my belly.

Tristan has just left, and Reece will be here soon. Kelly and Shelby are with me, and they have insisted that I wear a gown today. "You'll feel better if you look pretty," Kelly told me earlier when she asked me to put on the pink dress, but I don't know….

The bodice hardly covers anything. The sleeves are poofy, and the skirt is so full, I think there's enough material here to carpet the entire room.

I look silly. I look like one of those women on the cover of one of my romance books.

"You look beautiful!" Shelby insists as she finishes curling my hair. I hold still because I don't want her to burn me, but I don't know about any of this.

I definitely don't feel beautiful.

I feel like I might throw up, though.

I'm not sure what it is. I thought I was over the nausea that came with early pregnancy, but anymore, when I don't feel bored, I feel like the babies are warring inside of me. I'm starting to wonder if maybe I should go speak to Dr. Pindergoo, but I don't even know what I'd tell her except that I just don't feel right.

Maybe Emily did manage to poison me??

I shake my head. I'm just being stupid.

"Reece will be here in a few minutes," Shelby explains as she sets the curling iron down and unplugs it. I guess that means my hair is done.

"I hope he likes fluffy dresses," I mutter.

"He'll love it," Shelby assures me, and I see her exchange a giggle and a glance with Kelly, and I realize the two of them are up to something.

"What's going on?" I ask.

"Huh?" Kelly makes a face like she's innocent, and Shelby shrugs. I don't know what to say to either of them, so I only glare at them.

A few moments later, there's a knock at the door, and both of them laugh.

"See you later, Rose," Kelly announces.

"Have fun!" Shelby adds in a sing-song voice, and I have no doubt now that they are doing something behind my back.

The girls leave, but Reece doesn't come right in. Instead, he knocks again.

I fling the door open, wondering what's going on, and immediately, I freeze, my eyes wide with shock.

"Hello, my beautiful princess, Rose," he greets me, though it's a little hard to understand him—because he has a long-stemmed red rose clasped between his teeth. "I am here to ravish you!"

I take a step back and take him in.

He's wearing a long blue jacket with red trim, and it is unbuttoned completely. His pants aren't yellow like the book cover, but they're brown, and he has on black soldier boots. His hair is swept back with some kind of gel, and I can't spot a single hair on his chest anywhere.

And I am really looking.

"Wh-what's happening?" I ask as he comes in and closes the door behind him.

Reece whisks the rose out of his mouth and offers it to me. I'm not sure I want to take it. It's been in his mouth, after all.

But then… he's probably going to kiss me in a second, so I guess it's okay. I take the rose from him, and he pulls me to him, crushing me against his chest. "I can't live without you, beautiful woman," he declares in a voice deeper and huskier than the one that he usually uses.

"Uh, yeah, me neither," I reply, still taken aback.

Reece pushes away from me a little to put some space between us. "What's the matter, Rose?" he asks me. "I thought you'd like this. I heard about the book you were reading, and I thought it might be fun to role play. You don't like it?"

I realize then that he's gone to a lot of trouble to try to please me, and it makes me want to burst into tears because he's just so sweet. All of my men are. My emotions are all over the place, and I realize it has to be the babies and my hormones making me feel this way.

"Oh, Reece!" I exclaim. "It's wonderful. Thank you so much!" He pulls me back to him, kissing me deeply, and I suddenly feel like I am the woman on the cover of my book.

He takes his time, kissing me over and over again, rubbing his rough hands across my skin and setting it ablaze. The dress refuses to stay in place, and soon, my boobs are basically hanging out the top, which he takes advantage of. Reece massages my breasts, using his thumbs to rub my nipples into hardened peaks, before bending and taking me into his mouth. He sucks and licks until I toss my head back in euphoria.

As soon as I can control myself a bit, I take hold of his jacket lapels and pull them down sharply. For a moment, he is stuck in his jacket, and his hands have to come away from my breasts so we can get it off him. We both laugh, and he pulls his arms out. Then, he lifts me off my feet and carries me to the bed, depositing me on it with a longing look in his eyes, and the light from the candles Kelly and Shelby decorated the room with earlier is gleaming off Reece's perfectly polished chest.

He continues to take his time as he undresses both of us, one piece of clothing at a time.

Between shedding our attire, he kisses me deeply, sensually, and runs his tongue along my flesh. By the time we're both naked, I am already panting, longing for him.

He climbs atop the bed and positions himself between my legs. My belly is beginning to get in the way, but I want him so badly, I don't want him to stop.

Reece seems to notice this issue, too, so he pauses.

"We'll figure it out," I assure him, afraid he'll decide not to have sex with me after all.

"I know." He smiles down at me, and then, he moves around behind me, and at first, I'm not sure what he's doing, but then he rolls me onto my side, and I am now scissoring him, one leg over him, the other under him, and he is entering me sort of from… beneath.

It is a strange arrangement, one I can't quite grasp, but as he pushes inside of me, I also don't care. If I had to stand on my head for him to take me, I would do it–if I knew how.

In this position, I can't really see him, so I close my eyes and concentrate on how good it feels. He can reach my breasts and continues to play with them as he thrusts inside me over and over again, faster and faster. I can't do much to help him when I'm situated this way, but he doesn't need my help, and soon enough, I am floating above the clouds somewhere, everything about my body radiating pleasure.

This position must work well for Reece, too, because he begins to grunt once he's had me tipped into euphoria for several minutes, and then, he comes as well, and I feel his warmth shoot inside of me.

As soon as he's finished, he moves up next to me, pulling my back to his chest, and I wrap an arm through his, draping him over me.

"Did that feel okay?" he whispers in my ear.

"It felt amazing," I assure him, feeling him relax a bit at my comforting words. "That position was... different." I don't know how else to say it.

"I know," he agrees. "I read about it in a book, and I thought it might work well because of your baby bump."

"What book was that?" I ask *"The Kama Sutra for Pregnant People?"*

He laughs. "No, it was called, *How to Make Love When Your Woman is Prego,"* he explains.

I wonder if he would mind sharing the book with the other Alphas. As far as I can tell, none of the Alphas seem to have a problem sharing, which works in my favor.

Reece holds me close, and I feel sleepiness descending upon me. Any more, sleeping, eating, and having sex are about all I do. I wish my life was more exciting, especially since I know everything will change so drastically once the babies are born.

I try not to think about any of that now. If I think about what it will be like to give them away, I'll start crying, and Reece doesn't deserve to have to spend his precious time with me consoling me.

So I turn the tears off and think about how blessed I am to have these men in my life. Even if I never get to know their children, and I have to give them up soon as well, at least I have them now.

I decide to focus on that, focus on the now, and not on the hazy future that keeps rearing its ugly head through the mists.

It can wait for another day.

CHAPTER 16: WE DID NOT

"I am bored," I sulk.

Mark has brought me to his room. His bedroom has a beautiful window seat that faces the garden. I sit with his arms wrapped around my shoulders. Although the window is open, and I can feel the night air against my skin, this doesn't beat being physically outside.

He unwraps his arms from my shoulders and stands up.

"Okay. I have an idea. Why don't we do something exciting?" Mark asks.

I frown up at him. All my men have been trying to entertain me in very creative ways, but I am getting cabin fever from being cooped up in the house all the time. Today was better, as I had walked out of my room and down the hall to Mark's room. But I craved more.

"I am tired of sex games and old woman pantyhose," I reply dejectedly.

He raises a perfectly arched brow. "No. That's not what I have in mind. Just go to the door and make sure the hallway is empty. We are going on a secret escapade; I just need to grab something really quick."

My stomach churns, and I wonder if it's the anticipation of what Mark has planned, or if it was something else. I haven't been feeling well the last couple of days, but I reason it is just that boredom has overtaken me.

I stand up and feel my head spin for a second. I figure that I have stood up a little too quickly as the sensation quickly passes. I walk toward the door and poke my head into the hallway, looking right and then left, trying to stifle a giggle. I feel like a pregnant Velma Dinkle, about to embark on an adventure with the Scooby Doo gang. Except, it will just be Mark and myself.

"Coast is clear!" I hiss over my shoulder. Mark, who is holding pillows and a blanket, comes over, grabs my hand, and pulls me into the hallway.

We do a fast walk toward the door to the main hallway. A sudden dull jab in my stomach makes me freeze.

"Are you okay?" Mark is looking at me with worry in his eyes.

"Yes," I lie, not wanting whatever is happening with me to disrupt our adventure.

Mark puts his arm around my waist and slows his steps to a nonchalant stroll as we continue on our journey.

When we reach the stairs, he lets go of my waist. He stands with his back straight and a serious look printed on his handsome face.

"So," he says mildly as he bows lightly at me, "are you here for the ball, Miss...?"

Laughing, I stand straight and fan my face with my hand. "It's Lady Rose. And no, I am here with my man. I thought we would have fun tonight, but it seems he has abandoned me."

"Oh well, he sounds awful. Look, if you've given up looking for him, I was just about to go star gazing up on the roof if you'd care to join me?"

We both grin at each other as I clasp his hand and nod. Hands engaged, we walk up the spiraling staircase.

We get to an entryway, and I push the door open, longing to be outside. I hold it open with my arm and bow, "After you, my good sir."

"Why, thank you kindly," he replies.

As soon as the door closes behind us, I push past him and kick my shoes off, not bothering to pick them up as I make my way to the edge of the roof.

Mark follows me. I push myself up with my elbows on the ledge, my face thrust excitedly into the cool night air. It feels great to be outside.

Depositing bedding on the ground, Mark puts his arm around my protruding belly, nuzzling the back of my neck.

"So beautiful," I breathe.

"Mmm, and the view's not so bad either," he adds.

I turn around to face him. The look in his eyes tells me that he isn't talking about the scenery.

"Now that I've torn your eyes away from the beautiful night sky, to my handsome face, may I interest the lady in an under-the-stars dance? I call it the Mark dance."

Without missing a beat, he begins unbuttoning my shirt and noisily kissing and licking his way from my collarbone to my sternum. All the way down he follows the middle of my frame until he is on his knees at my feet.

I clasp my hands behind his head and look down into his blue eyes, which look more mischievous than usual.

"Well jeez, so this is the Mark dance?" I begin bending just a little to join him on the ground.

"Wait a minute. Mmm, you smell like cantaloupe," he murmurs, mouth muffled against my inner thigh. With both arms cupping the back of my legs, he continues to voice how good my skin tastes; he licks first along my left thigh, across my delicate cleft, and then back down the right.

Jutting his chin firmly under me, he looks up into my eyes, half closed with pleasure as I lean against the wall and hold onto the back of his head with my other arm.

"After thorough investigation, I have found that you are a unique and exotic dish that I wish to savor entirely."

I laugh and push his head gently back toward me. His tongue obliges, flat and pushing forward along my slit, then curling back as he pulls it upward to my most sensitive area. I shiver and place a knee on his shoulder as he delves forward and back, each time pausing longer to suck gently as I moan and squirm in his grasp.

I feel dizzy and lightheaded. My stomach churns in response. Suddenly, I'm not feeling so well, and it has nothing to do with him.

"Please, Mark. Stop," I declare, gently pushing him away.

"Oh, does the lady like that?" Mark asks playfully.

"No, really, stop," I plead.

"Can't handle the pleasure?"

A wave of nausea grips me, and I push him off, rushing toward the ledge. I bend over it and pour out the nasty-tasting liquid that is now lodged in my mouth.

"Hey, are there people up there?"

I freeze, blood thundering in my ears at the sound of a strange voice from below.

"Are you okay, baby?" Mark asks.

"No. I think I need to go see the doctor. Also, I think I just puked on someone down there," I say as I struggle to steady my legs.

"EVERYTHING IS ALL RIGHT. All the babies are fine as well, with strong heartbeats," Dr. Poundergone assures us.

I sigh in relief, and Mark squeezes my hand. I'm grateful that we found the doctor still in her office sorting out some files at this time of night.

"So why have I been feeling like sticky gum on a damp mop lately, doctor?"

"Hormones, dear. Your body is just adjusting. The flutters you're feeling could just be the babies moving. You are all right. Get fresh air often, drink a lot of clear fluids, and take everything slow," she says as she looks both Mark and me over. I feel my face heating up. I know she is talking about sex.

"Thank you, Doctor," Mark says. As we walk back to my room, Mark begins to snicker. "What do you think she meant by taking things slow?"

"You know exactly what she meant. We both look like we were put in one huge pan and tossed around," I reply as I look down at my bare feet and wiggle my toes.

"How are you feeling now?" Mark asks.

"Much better. I think the adrenaline got me flustered a bit there. Hey, who do you think I puked on down there?" I ask.

Mark shrugs. "What were they doing down there in the obscurity of the night anyway?"

"We were the ones sneaking around on the roof," I reason.

"They'll live. It was just vomit rain from the most beautiful woman in the world. They should feel honored," Mark chuckles and places a hand on the small of my back.

"Would you want me to puke on you?" I ask, my tone serious.

A crease forms between his brows. "I'll get the things we left up there later. For now, let's put you to bed."

I chuckle lightly, realizing that he just sidestepped my question.

When we reach my room, we get under the covers, and Mark spoons me.

"I think we had enough excitement for tonight. You need to rest. I will just snuggle with you tonight. No funny business," Mark affirms.

I snuggle closer to him. "I enjoyed our rendezvous. A pity the Mark dance had to be cut short. Rain check on it though. We'll put a 'to be continued' notice on it. We can't have you going to spank Emily for your release now, can we?"

He nuzzles my neck and snickers.

CHAPTER 17: A SWORD WITH TWO EDGES

M<small>ARK</small>

"It couldn't have been bird's poop. The stuff smelled like rancid egg fart in a jar. It soaked my hair and clothes. I had to shampoo my hair ten times just to get the smell off me. There was someone up there playing a sick prank on me."

I try to stifle my laughter as I pass Emily's room. She is complaining to her new chambermaid about last night, and I can only conclude she was the one Rose's puke landed on. How fitting! Rose had literally puked on her nemesis without even meaning to. The Moon Goddess has a great sense of humor.

"Hey, Marky-Mark? How was your night?" Eli asks when we gather to iron out the finer details about tonight. The Betas and Alphas are all set to show up soon to vie for Emily's affections.

"It was awesome. Rose puked on Emily's head," I say.

They all gape at me.

"What weird threesome BDSM party did you all have last night? Does Emily have a vomit fetish? Why wasn't I invited to this party? I am the king of weird shit!" Tristan announces.

I try to find where to start narrating the story, but I don't want them to know all the details about our secret rendezvous. "It wasn't intentional. No threesome either. With Emily? Gross. Rose vomited without knowing Emily was outside, then the vomit landed on Emily's head. Emily has no idea that it was Rose, though. So let's keep it that way."

They all make the sign of zipping their mouths.

"Although, I am still curious. How did Rose's vomit land on a person's head who was outside? Y'all were doing some weird shit, I'm telling you," Tristan probes as he waves a finger at me.

I shrug and smile cockily. "Well, details are of no importance right now. Just bask in the knowledge that the witch got herself some sweet vomit-rain."

~

I pass the day going through some papers, and catching up with everything that has been going on with my pack.

When I'm finally done, it's almost dusk. We all reconvene in Eli's room. As we are about to discuss tonight, there is a knock at the door, and Beta Adam walks in.

"The Alphas and Betas have started to arrive," he announces.

We all decide it's time to go welcome our guests.

"Do you think the king will have a fit when he finds out we organized all this without his knowledge and approval?" Reece asks.

"Huh, let him throw a tantrum even. Maybe the anger will make him grow an inch or two," Tristan exclaims.

Food and snack platters are arranged on the long dining hall table for a buffet-style meal. Carafes containing a range of wines are placed between the platters to fill the empty places. The plates, glasses, and cutlery have been set at each end of the table.

At one end of the hall, a dance floor has been established, set off with balloons and flowers.

There are some recognizable faces in the crowd. Some folks were there that I never would have guessed would be there.

I notice Alpha Morris standing in the room's corner. His mournful eyes dart around like a deer caught in headlights, and he stands with his shoulders hunched. With his lanky frame, he ought to continue moving about slumped over, in my opinion. The ceilings are high, but he could easily hit his head on some of the low-hanging chandeliers.

I can't help but wonder if he really thinks Emily would choose someone like him. Although he is an Alpha, something about his stature says frail and needy. Then again, Emily might love having a man she can control and dominate. Anything was possible; he could win her affection and shock us all.

"You stepped on my foot," Beta Eric is complaining loudly. We all turn to see Alpha Stephen towering over him and daring him to accuse him again.

"No, your foot got under mine. You should be the one apologizing," Alpha Stephen bellows at the poor Beta. Beta Eric cowers away from the menacing Alpha who has just entered.

"Who invited that evil jerk? I hate that guy. He is so vile… and so old. Do you remember the story about when he continuously ordered his chefs to be thrown into the dungeon all because they couldn't make his coffee right?" Eli asks.

"Yep. And I hear all his female staff have to sign on a big board whenever they start their periods. He wants to know so that they don't touch his food or are anywhere around him," Reece adds.

I can't help but frown, wondering what the reason for that would be. I don't have to voice my inquiry, as Tristan explains, "It's apparently because he says menstruating women have loads of drama. He now orders all of the female servants to stay on active birth control pills throughout their tenure in his household to block their periods. And he apparently has someone to check all women daily to ensure that they aren't having their period. If they're caught in the red zone, they're sent to the dungeons for a month and then fired right after."

I had always known he was a wicked man, but this was all too much to comprehend.

"He is so evil; he would be the perfect match for Emily. They are truly two of a kind," Eli recognizes. Before we can answer, he opposes his prior reasoning. "But that would be double the trouble and treachery."

"That's right. We need to find her a weakling who won't be a threat to anyone, especially not to Rose," I clarify.

"Ahh, how about Willy Wonka there?" Tristan asks as he gestures to Alpha Morris.

But suddenly, King Gene walks in with Emily hanging on his arm.

"What the hell is this ruckus? Who organized this in my palace without my permission?" he shouts, causing all the attendees to turn and glare at him.

Tristan steps in his direction. "Your Majesty, this is a ball we organized in honor of Miss Emily here."

Emily bats her long feathery lashes at Tristan. "I didn't request anyone to do such a thing," she argues.

"No, we did. We thought you deserve a ball to honor your, erm, beauty." He seems to struggle to say the last word.

"Oh, is that so?"

I can tell from the pink hue in her cheeks that she is flattered, but the red color on the king's face tells an opposing story.

"Who approved of this said plan?" King Gene demands.

"Oh, but don't you see? They did this for me. They're showing that they care for me for a change. Don't you want me to be happy, cousin?" This time she blinks rapidly at her cousin.

"Yes, but...." King Gene takes a few moments to ponder the situation before sighing. "Perhaps this will be a great opportunity to get some Alphas to side with us against Alpha Kane. At the very least, we could get to know who they ally themselves with, Alpha Kane or myself. I guess it could be beneficial to the pack."

We all nod and chorus how that was our thinking too.

Tristan offers his arm to Emily. "My lady," he says in his most charming voice. He then leads her toward Alpha Morris. After chatting with both of them a bit, he leaves Emily there and returns.

"I tried to give him a good playing field to win her. If he messes up the clear-cut scene I set for him, then he is really wonky. Not even a wizard will be able to save him," he jokes when he comes back to us.

"Maybe she won't fall for an Alpha from a pack as weak and small as the Sapling Pack," I say.

We give Alpha Morris some space to work his… magic… with Emily, and after a few minutes of gossiping about the night's attendees, Alpha Morris walks toward us with a defeated look etched on his scrawny facial features.

"She told me to go to hell and fuck fire. I guess I'm just not her type," he says, crestfallen, and then he walks toward the doors that lead into the garden dejectedly.

"You'll get 'em next time, big guy," Tristan shouts after him and nods his head resolutely.

"I think I should follow him, just to make sure he doesn't go hang himself from a tree or something," I say.

"Or drown himself in a chocolate fountain at his factory," Tristan adds.

I follow Alpha Morris. When I get outside, I look around to try to find him and see a figure standing at the entrance of the labyrinth. As I approach, I can hear him on the phone talking to someone excitedly. I frown as his mood shifts from sad to suddenly excited, which is perplexing.

As I near him, I overhear him say, "Hey, Father. I have great news that could have a positive impact on the future of our pack. I got a preposition from King Gene's cousin, Emily. She offered me one hundred thousand dollars to get rid of some Breeder and bring her back home to the pack house with me…."

CHAPTER 18: POSSIBILITIES ABOUND

EMILY

What the fuck is going on around here?

Why the hell are these Alphas holding a party in my honor? It doesn't make sense. Not that I don't love a good party, especially when I am the guest of honor, but none of that seems to fit because I knew that they all hate me.

Still... here I am wearing a fancy dress, the eyes of dozens of rich, handsome men on me, and I can't help but flutter my eyelashes and flirt with every man who comes my way.

"Well, you must be the beautiful Luna-to-be everyone has been telling me about."

I turn to see a handsome older man staring at me, his blue eyes narrowed as his gaze crawls the length of my body.

Silver fox is the only thing I can think of to describe him, despite the fact that I've got no doubt in my mind that he's a wolf in every sense of the word. His hair isn't even silver, not completely, just at the temples. But he's muscular, tan, and has the perfect features of a man who has always been a heartbreaker and knows it.

I can't help it when my hand reaches out to feel his bicep without even so much as a second thought.

"I am the Luna-to-be," I confirm in a confident voice. "I'm the queen-to-be, for that matter. And who, may I ask, are you?"

"Well, I'm surprised you don't already know," he says with a slight chuckle that makes my heart rate increase. "I'm Alpha Stephen."

"THE Alpha Stephen?" I have heard lots of stories about this man, not only about how strong his pack is but also about how he has a commanding presence in every sense of the word. In fact, I'm fairly certain that King Gene is afraid of him, frightened that he might one day try to take over the entire kingdom.

So... wouldn't it make sense for him to be the next in line for the throne?

I turn and look at the little boys who are part of this competition, and I can't help but wrinkle my nose up at them. They are all nothing but toddlers compared to Stephen. Sure, they're attractive, and I'm certain they're all good in the bedroom. But now that they've been with that awful Breeder, they're all a bit spoiled to me.

I know for a fact that Alpha Stephen has never had a reason for a Breeder. He had a Luna for many years who passed away, and now, he's available.

Available for a woman as beautiful and well-put together as I am.

"Care to dance?" He offers me his hand, and I slip my fingers into his palm. He leads me out onto the dance floor as a slow, romantic song starts, and we begin to sway in time to the music.

Our bodies are pressed together, and for a few moments, with my eyes closed, I think that I know what it would be like to make love to this man.

I can't wait to find out....

"So, tell me about this competition," he begins the conversation. "You're to wed the Alpha who gets the Breeder pregnant, right?" His voice is a low grumble of pleasure that ignites my core.

I nod. "That was the plan, but my understanding is that the bitch is carrying four babies, one for each of them."

"That sounds like a problem," he says with a mild chuckle.

I nod again. "It is. But King Gene is trying to come up with another solution, one that will get around the clause that says that only one of them can become the next king, the one that knocked her up first."

"Surely, he's not thinking of splitting the kingdom," Alpha Stephen asks without asking.

I shake my head. "I don't think he'd ever do that."

"Good. That would just make us weak, and our enemies would be ready to pounce on the kingdom. It's bad enough he's let someone like Alpha Kane rise up against him already."

Alpha Stephen seems to know an awful lot about what's going on in the kingdom. I am impressed, and while I can't tell if he's flirting with me because he wants to be the next king or if he is genuinely interested in me, he's hot, and I'm certain he's good in bed. The fact that he's not tainted by that awful Breeder puts him ahead in my book.

I don't really care who I marry so long as they check all of those boxes, and I still get to be queen. "We should go talk to my cousin," I suggest when the song is over and something faster begins to play. I don't feel like getting my groove on just now.

"Talk to your cousin?" Alpha Stephen repeats. He has stopped dancing, along with me, but his hand is still gripping mine. "About what, Emily, dear?"

"About... things." I'm not sure how specific I should be at this point. "Come on." I give his hand a tug and start walking before I even establish where my cousin has gone.

I glance around the room, but I don't see King Gene anywhere. I can hear his voice, though, so I follow the sound of his grating words to the area where the food is set up. He is talking to a group of older Alphas, ones old enough to be Alpha Stephen's father, and I am wondering why these men are even here. Were the other four Alphas trying to marry me off to an old grandpa?

If I'm going to have a baby that will be the heir instead of one of the stupid Breeder babies, at least provide me with a man that I actually want to have sex with.

"Cousin," I whisper, coming up next to the king.

He turns and looks at me like I am interrupting something very important. I have no idea what they were talking about, and I don't care. I am the most important person here. This is my party. Nothing else matters.

"What do you want?" he barks at me, his eyes narrowing like I'm interjecting myself into the middle of a conversation that cannot be put off.

"Do you know Alpha Stephen?" I ask him.

King Gene shakes his head in annoyance. "Do you honestly think there's an Alpha in this kingdom I don't know?" he asks me in the gruff voice that he reserves for yelling at staff members.

I can't help but glare at him. "This is my party," I remind him. "Whatever you're talking about, I bet it can wait until later."

"The state of the kingdom?" one of the grandpa Alphas asks me. "You think your little celebration is more important than potential war?"

"Listen, old man," I begin, a hand on my hip, "maybe you don't know who I am, or maybe you're too senile to remember, but yes, right now, I am more important than anything else. This is my party. A celebration of me, and if you came here under some false pretenses to try to get a moment with the king, I will remind you that you are talking to the king's cousin!"

The old man stares at me, his mouth agape, his eyes wide, as he begins to try to say something about how offended he is, but King Gene excuses himself, takes my arm, and leads me away.

Alpha Stephen follows along.

"Emily, what in the world is it?" he asks, his tone conveying he is tired, not annoyed.

That's what I tell myself, anyway.

"Well, I just thought…. You know, those four Alphas you originally chose are acting like spoiled brats. They keep running around behind your back, trying to make it so that that stupid Breeder seems more important than she is, more important than I am, and I am almost positive they are trying to undermine your authority as well."

"What is your point, Emily?" King Gene asks me, folding his arms across his chest.

"My point is, I think it's time to call this whole thing off. Let's just get rid of that stupid Breeder once and for all, and all of these stupid Alphas. Let me marry a real man, someone who can get me pregnant, and then the heir will really be related to you!"

"And who in their right mind would want to marry you?" King Gene asks. I am offended for a moment before I realize I already have an answer to that question.

We both turn to look at Alpha Stephen. He looks slightly confused and maybe a little overwhelmed, but then he asks, "Did someone say... future king?"

"I don't think that's exactly what I said," King Gene replies. "But tell me, Alpha Stephen, are you interested in possibly marrying Emily?"

Alpha Stephen looks at me, and I think I see his throat move as he swallows. When he speaks, it's only one word.

"Probably."

Well, at least that wasn't a no. I might be able to work with this.

CHAPTER 19: MORRIS IS SCARED

Mark

The moment Alpha Morris hangs up the phone, I'm on him.

His eyes bulge as he sees me flying at him, my hands still in the pockets of my suit pants. "Morris?" I ask, biting my lip for a second to keep from losing my cool. "What the fuck did I just hear you say?"

His eyes bulge slightly, and he says, "Oh, nothing. I was just talking to… a friend. About… a television show." He tries to smile at me, but he's not fooling me.

Not even a little bit.

My hand clamps down on his shoulder, and I say, "I really don't think that you were."

Even in the darkness of the garden at night, I can see the beads of sweat popping out all over his forehead. "No, you know, I… uh…."

I steer him back toward the party, but not for more dancing or speaking to Emily. I think we've had plenty of opportunities to chat with that bitch, so I keep right on walking. I see Emily and Gene talking with Alpha Stephen, and I start to perk up a little, but then I remember what I overheard.

Morris has it in his head that he can kill Rose.

"Where are we going, Alpha Mark?" Morris asks as I continue to walk, moving him alongside me.

"Well, I just figured you thought it would be so easy to earn that money and do what Emily asked you to do, so maybe I'd just help you out," I tell him, seething as I guide him down the hallway.

"I really think you misunderstood," he tries again, but I don't want to hear it. I know what I heard.

We reach Eli's room, and I knock on the door, hard.

"What's the password?" I hear Kelly's voice through the wooden door.

Taking a deep breath, I realize I'm about to sound silly in front of an Alpha I'm trying to rough up. "Boom shakalaka," I say in my most menacing voice.

"Shakalaka laka?" Kelly asks.

I see Morris's brow furrow as I take a deep breath and reply, "Shakalaka laka laka, boom."

Kelly cracks the door open just a bit so I can see one eye. "You forgot a laka, Mark."

"Just open the damn door," I demand with a sigh.

She does, convinced it's me now, and not some murderer. Although, I suppose I have brought the would-be murderer with me.

"Who's the stiff?" she asks as I guide Alpha Morris inside. He clears his throat and runs his free hand nervously through his hair. He can't move his other arm because I am still clamped down on his shoulder.

"This is Alpha Morris." I push him down into a chair across from where Rose is sitting on the couch with yarn and some kind of long, metal hook thingy in her hand. "He wants us to call him Killer, though, because he's a tough guy."

"Who's a tough guy?" Eli comes in behind us.

"You didn't lock the door behind us?" I ask Kelly, more concerned that he didn't have to stay that stupid password than the fact that he just strolled right in.

Kelly shrugs. "Neither did you."

Eli turns to lock the door, but before he can do so, we hear a thunderous, "Boom shaka laka!"

"Just let Tristan in," I instruct. "Is Reece behind him?"

"No, I left him to guard Emily," Tristan says as he tries to slide through the crack Eli's left in the door, which isn't nearly big enough, and he ends up pushing the door, and Eli, backward a couple of feet.

I shake my head and try not to roll my eyes. "Lock it," I command.

"From... the inside?" Morris asks. He's sweating even worse now than he was before.

"You don't wanna be locked in here with us either way," I assure him.

"Mark, baby, what's going on?" Rose asks, and the sound of her sweet voice has me wanting to run to her. I can't help but get up and walk over to kiss her. I sit down next to her, accidentally knocking her ball of yarn off of the couch. It unrolls as it takes off across the floor, hiding beneath Eli's bed.

"Sorry," I mumble.

"It's fine," she assures, setting the rest of what she was holding down on the coffee table. "I'm not getting the hang of crocheting anyway."

"Crotchet-ing?" Tristan says, butchering the word. "I can help you with your crotch, little flower. Whatcha need?"

"That's not what she said," I tell him, glaring at him. "Listen, you guys, I just overheard Morris talking to someone on the phone back at his pack, his dad, maybe? Anyway, Emily tried to make a deal with him, one he's going to regret ever considering."

"I... I'm not considering it," Morris refutes, wiping the sweat that's pouring down his forehead onto his sleeve. "I would never ever... it was just... my pack needs the money, that's all."

"What were you supposed to do?" Rose asks him, and I squeeze her hand, waiting for him to answer.

"It's nothing, Miss–" Morris stops, a confused look on his face.

I gesture to Rose's stomach. "Morris, this is Rose," I tell him. "Your prey."

"What?" Rose asks, her eyes wide. I wrap an arm protectively around her as she turns her attention back to Morris. "What does that mean?"

"It doesn't... I mean, I never...." He takes a deep breath, clears his throat, and runs a hand through his hair.

Tristan clamps both of his giant hands on either of Morris's shoulders. "Why don't you go ahead and tell us what Emily wanted, Morrsey, before I decide to snap your head off?" he prompts.

Morris's mouth is open, but no sounds are coming out as the sweat spews off of him. It looks like he has a fire hose hidden in the back of his shirt.

Tristan comes around the front and crouches down in front of him. "We can do this the easy way, or the hard way. Don't make me go get my magic wand."

"M-magic wand?" Morris stammers.

"That's right. You're gonna wish you never met it once you lay an eye on it, so why don't you tell us what Emily wanted you to do?" His voice is calm, but I can see that the back of Tristan's neck is about to explode from the tension in his muscles and tendons.

In a soft voice, Morris confesses, "Emily offered me money to... kill... the Breeder... and her babies."

"Our babies," I clarify.

I hear Eli swear behind him.

"But I never would have done it!" Morris exclaims, pleading with Tristan.

"No, of course, you wouldn't have," Tristan says. "And if I ever hear another word about it, I'll shove my magic wand so far up your ass you'll be singing soprano."

"I've seen his magic wand," Rose chimes in. "You don't want it anywhere near your ass."

Morris looks petrified, and I'm not sure if his sweat just smells like urine or if he's peed himself a little.

"D-don't worry," Alpha Morris stammers. "I would never hurt an innocent woman."

"Not this one you won't," Eli says as he comes to stand behind

Tristan, his arms folded across his chest. "We will snap you in half like a twig."

"I understand," Morris says. "Believe me... I will never, ever be a problem for any of you or for Miss Rose."

We stare him down for a moment, and then Eli says, "Get the fuck out of my room."

Without having to be told twice, Morris shoots up out of the chair, taking off toward the door, shouting behind him as he throws it open, "Boom shakalaka!"

"Goddess... Emily's never going to stop, is she?" Rose is beginning to cry, and I feel terrible that she's upset. I shouldn't have brought him here. I just needed to get Morris away from the other Alphas so I could intimidate him more easily.

Pulling her to my chest, I tell her, "Don't worry, Rose. She will once she realizes she can't win. Besides, I saw her talking to another Alpha, and I think she might actually be interested in him."

Rose's face brightens at the possibility. "Do you really think there's a chance she might find someone else to focus on? But then, King Gene would have to agree with him becoming king, and then none of you will be. And... well, it all seems like such a complex mess."

"It is complex, but we'll figure it out," I assure her. I press my lips to the top of her head, hoping I've soothed her some.

She looks up at me and smiles. "I trust you."

"Good." I brush her tears away. "She's out there dancing with Alpha Stephen right now, and with any luck, she'll fall in love with him, and he'll take her away. Then, we won't have to worry about Emily anymore."

I know it's a long shot, but I have to believe we'll find a way to pull this off. I can't let anything happen to Rose and the babies.

CHAPTER 20: COULD IT WORK?

Tristan

I LISTEN to Mark trying to convince Rose that everything is going to be all right, but I'm not completely sure he's convincing her.

He isn't convincing me. We still have a lot left to do.

Before I can suggest that we get back to the dance, Eli says, "Alpha Stephen is a notoriously evil man. I'm not sure that having Emily team up with him is really the way to go."

"Well, we'll just have to make sure they hook up and get as far away from the castle as possible so that they aren't where they can hurt Rose or the babies," Mark adds.

"We need to get back there," I declare. "We've left Reece holding down the fort for long enough. We've got to make sure we can convince Gene to send Emily off to marry Stephen or whoever without it making a problem for us."

"Are you okay with us leaving again?" Eli asks Rose.

"Yes, of course," she assures us. "If that's what it takes for this plan to work."

Mark kisses her on the right cheek, Eli kisses her on the left cheek, and I wait for them both to move before leaning down and kissing her sweet lips.

"Really, Tristan?" Mark asks, his panties in a wad again.

"Well, I can't help it if you guys carry your balls in bowling ball bags. Let's go."

Rose giggles, and I wink at her.

The others head toward the door, and I follow along. Kelly is on our heels, ready to lock up behind us.

"See you later, beautiful!" I call, giving Rose a little wave. The others say something sweet, too, but I'm too busy staring at her lovely face to catch it.

We walk down the hallway together, back toward the ballroom. "This plan isn't going to work the way that you want it to," Eli tells Mark. "If anything, King Gene will have Alpha Stephen stay and marry Emily, and the rest of us will get booted out."

"Well, then, we'll just have to fight to stay," I say before Mark has a chance to respond.

"Why would we do that?" Mark asks. "Let's just take Rose somewhere safe and be done with it."

"No way," I refute, shaking my head. "Our babies are meant to be royals one day. We can't take that away from them."

"Our babies will be better off in any other occupation," Mark shoots back.

I want to continue to argue with him, but we have arrived in the ballroom, and it turns out that the other Alphas are leaving.

"What's happening?" I ask, jumping between a few of them and the door.

"Sorry, Alpha Tristan," one of them, Alpha Dan, apologizes. "We see that Emily is preoccupied." He claps me on the shoulder. "It's just as well. That girl is a bitch!" he adds quietly.

"But... did you even dance with her?" I ask, trying to chase Alpha Dan and the others down. It does me no good. They are leaving.

At least Alpha Stephen is still here. He's dancing with Emily, and King Gene is talking to a couple of the other more sinister Alphas. Maybe we still have a chance at marrying the murdering bitch off.

Reece is talking to Mark and Eli, and it looks like he's filling them in on what we missed, and possibly they are also telling him the same about what he missed from what happened in Eli's room.

"So Emily actually tried to bribe Morris into killing Rose?" Reece is saying as I approach.

"That's right," Mark tells him. "What are the chances that she didn't approach any of the other Alphas and try to pay them off to kill her as well?"

"Do you think anyone else is desperate enough to try to do that?" Eli asks.

"I hope not," Mark replies. "We'll have to be extra diligent for the next few days."

I sigh, my hands pushed down in my pockets, and gaze around the dance floor. Even the band seems bored. They're playing a version of a rock song I think I recognize, but it's so slow and somber, it sounds more like a death march or a funeral dirge.

The place still looks nice, even if that's probably because half of the room wasn't even used. Only about thirty people were here, and this room fits hundreds. Kelly and Shelby did a great job setting up the tables, but even the flowers in the centerpieces look like they are bored. They seem to be staring down at the silver tablecloths like they are reaching for the sun.

Or just hiding their faces.

I notice that Alpha Stephen and Emily are approaching Gene now, and the other Alphas that were standing around him take off, leaving the three of them together to discuss... whatever it might be that Emily thinks she's convinced Alpha Stephen to do.

"What do you think they're talking about?" Reece asks, trying not to stare at the trio.

"I'm not a betting man, but if I were, I'd put my money on them discussing whether or not Alpha Stephen is good king material," Eli hypothesizes.

"I hope so," Mark adds. "It would be great if this could all be over soon. I'm getting really tired of people threatening Rose's life."

"Well, there's only one way to find out," I say. A waiter walks by with a few glasses of champagne. I pluck one off and down it before I head over to where Gene, Emily, and Stephen are chatting.

"Tristan!" I hear Mark growl, but I ignore him. He's not the boss of me, and I can do whatever I please.

I walk over to them and clap Stephen on the shoulder. "Hey, old buddy!" I say with a fake grin. "You sure look nice tonight for... an old guy. For a–" I clear my throat when I see his eyebrows shoot up. "For a guy. That's... old."

"What do you want, Tristan?" King Gene growls at me like I'm interfering in his very important discussion.

"Nothing. I just wanted to come over and see what's going on, that's all. Emily is our guest of... honor." I have to clear my throat before I choke that last word out. She doesn't seem like she should ever be the guest of honor at anything, not even her own funeral.

"Alpha Stephen and I have hit it off," Emily announces with a flirtatious smile. "He's very kind and loving. Unlike... some people I know. And I was just discussing with my uncle how it doesn't seem fair that Alpha Stephen, the most powerful Alpha in our kingdom, wasn't considered to be the next king."

"That is a strange situation," I rub my chin, mockingly. "Well, I'm sure King Gene had a good reason." Although, I'm sure he doesn't, because he never has a good reason for anything.

"Yes, I did," King Gene replies, rocking back and forth from his heels to his toes. "As Alpha Tristan so eloquently put it, Alpha Stephen is old. I wanted a young Alpha to provide an heir and to become the husband to my cousin. But... with all of the shenanigans going on around here, well, Emily makes some good arguments for why it would make sense for me to have an older Alpha take over after me."

"And for me to have my own heir!" Emily pouts, folding her arms and sticking out her bottom lip.

"Yes, yes, but as I've told you before, it is important to me for you to maintain your virtue, my dear cousin." King Gene says with his face so straight, I almost choke trying not to laugh.

He really thinks that Emily is a virgin?

I will have to excuse myself since I can't stand here and listen to this much longer. "Well, Emily, I hope you get someone that deserves you... someone that you deserve."

She looks at me like I have said something touching. "Thank you, Alpha Tristan. I always thought you were too good for that disgusting Breeder bitch."

"And... this is where I leave you." I turn around and walk away so I don't ram my fist through her chest, pluck out the black lump of coal that is her heart, and shove it up her ass.

When I reach the other Alphas, I am breathing deeply, and I have mostly calmed myself. "Well?" Eli asks.

I nod. "She's working on it. She's trying to convince Gene that he should let her have her own heir and that Stephen should be the father and the next king."

"But that's not what we want!" Reece exclaims.

"Listen, you're not going to have it both ways," Mark tells him. "Let's just focus on getting Emily married off to someone else. Then we'll worry about the rest of it, the babies being kings and queens and all of that, all right?"

I take a deep breath, hold it, and then slowly blow it out. I tend to agree with Reece. I'm not ready to hand all of this over to Alpha Stephen, but I do agree that making sure that Rose and the babies are safe is our first priority.

Then... we'll have to worry about everything else.

CHAPTER 21: FATHER KNOWS BEST–OR DOES HE?

Emily

It has been two months of daily usage of one of the wands in my drawers, two months since my last toe-curling orgasm from a man. I watch as the attendees of my party begin to depart. I can't let Alpha Stephen go. I need him to take care of a delicate itch only a cock is built to scratch.

Tonight is the night I can finally have the big 'O' I have been dreaming about. I want it to be amazing; I have waited for so long. It would be a shame to let this man, who was looking at me like I'm the best thing he has seen since the invention of sliced bread, walk away.

I have dreamt about it; an Alpha's rod buried deep inside of me, the feeling of his seed filling me up as I tumble over the edge and enjoy the full ecstasy of pleasure.

It's a pity they haven't made vibrators that can mimic the feeling of a man reaching their release. The feeling of fully dominating a man is what truly gets me going. I want to know that I'm powerful enough to biologically drain a man of all his intimate juices by just clenching my inner muscles and blowing in his ear.

"Emily...!" he will scream, and I will know I hold all the power.

Well, not that I need a man to tell me how good I am in bed; I already know that. I am Emily, after all. In school, they called me Egotistical Emily. I thought it was an insult until some of the boys told me it was a name born of praise at how good I was in bed. All the boys knew that, of course. They had all tasted my honey pot and knew just how sweet it was.

King Gene would have a fit if he knows that I plan to ask Alpha Stephen to spend the night with me. He thinks I'm this pure, innocent girl who still thinks men and women have the same genitalia. I can't help but roll my eyes.

I lost my virginity at fifteen to the driver's son who used to chauffeur me everywhere. He was a kid and couldn't satisfy me, so as time went on, I turned my attention to his father. He was okay, but still couldn't reach his dick to the core of my need.

Alpha Stephen is older, and I'm sure he has so much experience. If anyone knew which buttons to press and which knobs to twist, it would be him.

"Alpha Stephen, why don't you spend the night here? Just get a feel of how it is to live within the royal walls, so to speak." I wink at him, hoping he gets a sense of what I am hinting at by 'royal walls.'

He blinks at me, and I feel the need to wink again to drive the point across.

"Did something lodge in your eye, Miss Emily?" he asks.

Heck! Couldn't the man get a subtle hint?

"No. I am asking you to spend the night with me. No need to beat around the bush, right?" I wink at him again.

The wrinkles in his forehead deepen as he regards me. "I really think there is something wrong with your eyes. They keep twitching. Do you need me to take a look?"

I want to scream, "Come and fuck me, you old fool!" I smile sweetly instead, although at this point trying to be sexy and inviting is getting tiring. The idiot is not getting any of my hints. Also, if I scream, my cousin will come back to ask what's going on. I have to keep the myth of my purity alive, at least in his eyes.

I look over my shoulder and see that he's busy talking with the four Alphas and Beta Adam. They look very engrossed in whatever they're talking about. The Alphas, however, keep looking in my direction and smiling. I wonder if my showing interest in Alpha Stephen was making them jealous.

"Spend the night," I request again to Alpha Stephen.

"I need to go home and take care of some things," he replies.

"Come on. It's late, what will you possibly do at this hour?" I ask, and this time run a finger down his arm suggestively. This action seems to make him see what it is I was actually offering.

"Oh. All right. You are right, Miss Emily. It is rather late. Will you please lead the way to the chambers I will be spending the night in?"

I smile my approval at him. With one last look toward my cousin, who seems oblivious to the porn that was about to go down right underneath his roof, I take Alpha Stephen's arm and walk with him to my room.

"Miss Emily, is this your torture chamber? I have one back home, but I keep mine in the dungeons. Why would you have yours in the room you sleep in? Oh, do you also like torturing your servants and chambermaids when they add too much milk to your coffee? Or if the steak is not cooked through?"

I turn to look at Alpha Stephen, who is eyeing my bedroom with a weird smile on his somewhat confused face. I think my face looks equally confused. What was he going on about?

"No. I want you to torture me with pleasure. This is my heaven," I say proudly.

He again looks at me confused. "Why would I torture you? You're not on your period, are you?"

I raise my eyebrow at him, wondering what he was talking about again. Did he have a fetish for sleeping with women on their periods? Ew!

"No. Come in." I pull him into the room and close the door. The drapes are closed. I light the red candles around the room. I've been told that a red flame charges the atmosphere with sexual energy. I turn off the lights, and the candle flames illuminate the dim room.

121

"Make yourself comfortable. I'll be right back," I declare and go to my bathroom to get into my gear.

I'm back within a few minutes. He is sitting on the bed and has removed his shoes, but nothing else. He gazes at me; I see an intense look pass over his features, and he swallows.

I'm standing in the middle of the room wearing nothing but my favorite pair of red heels and a black body harness. I've rubbed coconut oil all over my body, and I know my exposed gorgeous skin looks sleek and begs to be caressed. My breasts are perked up, waiting for the firm grasp of his hands. I sway my hips....

"Surprised, I see," I smile at him.

He continues to stare and nods.

"Don't just sit there, Daddy. Show me the goodies," I coax.

He raises a finger and then takes out a bottle of pills from his pockets. He pops one into his mouth. I pray he isn't on some type of heart medication.

"What was that?" I ask.

"Just a magic pill to make this night amazing," he explains.

"You need pills to get a hard-on? Even after seeing all this?" I ask disgustedly, as I run my hands down my body.

He stands up and begins to remove his clothes without bothering to answer me.

He stands in front of me, hands on his hips, naked with a smug look on his face. We stand in silence as I take in his frame. His body is so wrinkled, it looks like it could use good steam iron treatment all over it. A shriveled, flaccid rod lies limply down a huge scrotum. What in the crown jewels is this?

I want to tell him to just leave, but I really need to get some kind of release tonight. I'd have to make do with this.... Oh my, his shaft really looks like an old used condom.

"How long will it take for your, erm, magic pill to kick in?" I ask.

He smiles widely at me. "Just a few jogs should get the blood flowing to the right places, sweet Em." With that, he begins jogging in one spot. The action causes his limp flesh to jiggle about, and his deflated prick bounces on his thigh making a slapping sound. Nothing about this looks sexy.

I swallow my repulsion. "Tie me up and spank me." I move toward the bed.

When I get to him, he pushes me roughly onto the bed. "No need to tie you up. I am ready, and we should do this before the magic disappears."

What in the royal fuck? As I lie on my back, he nudges my thighs apart and spits right into my intimate spot. He straddles me, pinning my body down with his weight. I can feel something soft and squishy probing my apex. Was that as hard as he was going to get?

He grinds up and down my body, and I wonder when he will actually penetrate me. He starts groaning and asking if I can feel him. Feel what? Nauseated? What is he doing?

"Do you like that, dear?" he whispers breathily into my ear. He puts an arm on top of my head and tucks my face under his hairy armpit. My nostrils are filled with the smell of sweat and garlic. The hairs in his pit tickle my face and sometimes get into my mouth.

One hand comes up to his lips, then I feel him stick a wet finger into my ear. Is this guy giving me a wet willy? What gave him the idea that that is sexy? However, the finger in my ear is fucking it more than his rod is doing to my neither regions. I really envy my ear right now.

"Ahhh!" he shouts and then rolls off to the side. What has just happened? Is he done? I put my hand down to see if I am wet from his seed, but I can't feel anything. Is he so old the liquid has dried up already, and he now only shoots out powder instead?

"That was wonderful. Did you like that? Of course, you did. Daddy knows just how to give it to you right. I felt you shivering, huh. I know I still got it!"

I scrunch up my nose. What is he talking about? What has just happened? I lay on my back speechless. Emily is never speechless... but this sex, if it can be called that, has left my vocabulary as dry as his sexual act.

I don't know if I want to marry this old geezer. He might be powerful out there, but in bed, he is just like a rooster. He just jiggles his wrinkles and flaps his loose flesh for five minutes, then grinds a non-existent dick on me for a minute… and done.

Egotistical Emily isn't about to marry a rooster of a man. I need satisfaction, not this weird shit.

CHAPTER 22: THREE MAN TASK FORCE

Eli

We all watch as the king taps his fingers on the windowsill, looking out over the fertile green lands of the prosperous kingdom. Prosperous, happy, and headed for absolute disaster if we don't win this war and stop Alpha Kane.

The battle line is engraved deep in the sand, and Alpha Kane isn't backing down. His threats have been made more real when he sent some shifters from his pack to attack the student healers in the woods as they gathered some herbs for their medicinal potions. The attack was unexpected and brutal, and the message was clear: Alpha Kane is willing to spill any and all blood to show his wrath and prove his strength.

"I need the four of you to be in the front of the battle line. Why are none of you in the front on this formation plan you just showed me?" King Gene asks.

"The formation we're opting for is more effective. If they think that you only sent the royal soldiers, they'll relax, not knowing that we're right in the middle. We'll have the element of surprise on our side," Mark replies.

The king stops and turns to face us. "Ahh, you will have the element of surprise on your side. They won't see you coming. I think this is the best plan I have ever thought of."

Wait, what? Had he suddenly adopted our plan as his own?

"Yes, it seems you do have fabulous plans, Your Majesty," Tristan cheers, not caring to hide the hint of sarcasm in his voice.

"We have one request, though. Rose is carrying our children. We can't all possibly go to war and leave her alone. If anything should happen to us, we need someone here to protect her," I add.

A dark shadow passes over the king's face. "The Breeder will be fine. I need the four of you on the battlefield. She is safe here. I will make sure to put the best guards on duty to protect these walls and everyone within them."

"We fear the real danger is within these very walls," Tristan utters. I smirk.

"Did you say something?" the king asks him.

"Nope. So, are you going to be in the front or the back of the battle line?" Tristan inquires. It seems Tristan just woke up today and chose violence.

"I am not going to fight. I will stay here and man this station as king. The people need me. We can't have the king going to war and dying." he answers.

"I see," Tristan responds.

I frown. Talk about double standards.

WE ALL SIT in different places in Eli's room as we try to come up with a plan to make sure we don't leave Rose without a proper guard. The king is adamant about the four of us going to war, but that will leave Rose without our protection.

"We can't all go," Mark states.

"When we leave, the king will do a head count if he has to, to make sure that we all go," Reece counters.

"We need a plan. Rose will be at the mercy of Emily and her cousin if we all go," Mark points out.

"Excuse me, we're here. I bought a new pair of nun chucks that will deter any attack, I assure you," Kelly argues, as she nods her head toward Shelby.

"Yeah, we're here. I don't know about fighting with nunchucks, but I do pack a mean punch. Emily's Botox-filled face won't know if I hit her with a hammer or rock," Shelby jokes as she balls her small hand into a fist and blows on it menacingly.

"The two of you are great fighters, don't get me wrong. But, what happens when Shelby is busy making her Adam sing soprano, or when Kelly is busy shopping for a new pair of boots? You need extra help," Tristan insists.

I smile as I notice Shelby blushing.

"So, what do you plan on doing? Unless one of you has a cloak of invisibility, I don't see how you can stay here unnoticed by the king or anyone else for that matter," Kelly explains her concern.

"Say, Tristan, don't you have an invisibility cloak in your bag of tricks?" I ask.

"I wish. It would have been a great thing to have in my college days. Imagine sneaking into the girls' locker rooms unnoticed," he says, deadly serious, and I shake my head.

"Reece can stay behind," Mark suggests.

"Why me?" Reece asks.

"You'd be the perfect person to protect Rose back here," Mark explains.

"Do you think I'd be useless on the battlefield?" Reece asks, sounding angry at the suggestion.

"As a matter of fact, your job will be the most taxing. Emily and her cousin are sneaky and even more dangerous. If you were to be discovered defying the king by staying back, you would be in immense trouble. Also, Rose is the most priced treasure who we are trusting you to guard," Mark assures him as he gives Rose a sideways glance and winks at her.

"The king will still expect to see the four of us leaving this castle, not three," Reece points out.

"You're right," I agree, and I hope someone will come up with a workable solution to execute this plan.

"Reece will leave with us, but then turn back and return to Rose. He'll alert her that he's outside her window, and she'll open it so that he can climb in," Tristan says.

"I would have to sneak in back here unnoticed. Shouting boom shakalaka laka from outside to get her to open the window will not be inconspicuous," Reece counters.

"How about you be a Romeo? I mean out of all of us, you're the most romantic, yet you couldn't think of the most romantic scene in Romeo and Juliet? Throw some small pebbles at her window to let her know you're outside. Just don't shout 'Juliet, oh where art thou, Juliet?'" Tristan suggests.

We all turn to look at Tristan. Who would have thought Tristan knew who Romeo and Juliet were?

"Hey, I studied the book in school. In case you didn't know, I minored in literature. If you want to speak the love language fluently, study literature." He shrugs.

"That's so romantic," the three ladies coo as they look at him with admiration. Even without the help of his toys, he can make girls weak. I roll my eyes.

"But we would need to make him look unrecognizable, in case someone sees him around the palace. He would have to blend in," Shelby adds.

"I thought we figured that none of us has a cloak of invisibility. How will we make me somewhat invisible?" Reece asks.

Shelby and Kelly exchange a look and smile brightly at Reece. His eyes dart from one lady to the other.

"Guys, I'm scared," he whimpers.

"Makeover!" the girls all scream at once.

I plant my face into my palm. The poor guy is in trouble. I'd grown up with Kelly, and she'd always practiced her make-up skills on me. I remembered the hard patting with a sponge on my poor skin, all in the name of blending, and the uncomfortable glide of the eyeliner on my eyelids. Being told to sit still or she would mistakenly take out my eye hadn't made the experience any sweeter. How did women do that to themselves every day?

"We'll all wait in Rose's room for your return. We'll gather some servant clothes and make you look just like one of them," Shelby says excitedly.

"Oh, we'll also need a wig to hide that hair," Kelly says.

"What do you think? Dreadlocks?" Shelby asks.

Kelly studies Reece for a bit. "No, his face has a round shape. Dreadlocks won't look nice on him. Maybe a nice bowl cut wig?"

"Yeah, that could work. And some dark brown contact lenses. Do you think he'll need some prosthetics? Maybe for his nose and cheekbones?" Shelby asks as she folds her arms across her chest, studying Reece like he's a science project.

"No. He won't need a prosthetic for his nose. It is already big. We could make it smaller by shaving it down with some dark contouring," Kelly offers.

Reece puts a hand to his nose. "Shave my nose? As in cut it?"

We're all watching, holding in our laughter.

"What shade do you say we use as a foundation? We can't keep his natural tone, though. Maybe make him look a bit paler. Servants are indoors most of the time and don't have the honey tone his skin has." The girls continue talking, ignoring Reece, who looks terrified.

"Yes. A pale foundation will make shaving his nose down easier," Kelly agrees.

Reece looks at us, his eyes open wide. "Help."

CHAPTER 23: AN ALPHA UNDERCOVER

Reece

I keep having to do a double-take each time I pass in front of a mirror or reflective surface. I always heard girls say makeup was supposed to enhance a person's beauty. This makeup wasn't enhancing anything about me; it just makes me look like a total stranger with ridiculously high cheekbones.

I touch my nose as I realize how small it appears, but when I grasp it, I can tell it is still the same size. Makeup can really create illusions. I'm glad, however, that shaving my nose down didn't mean cutting it off.

Shelby and Kelly are out making arrangements for the surprise baby shower they plan to throw for Rose. I was told to keep my lips sealed tight about it or else Kelly will shove the toe of her boot up my behind. I plan to keep quiet about the surprise as I doubt she was joking about the consequences.

I walk over to where Rose is sitting, reading yet another romance novel.

"How many of those do you read per day?" I ask, genuinely curious. When she looks up at me, her eyes widen for a split second, and she giggles.

"You look so different that I keep getting surprised every time I see you. I keep thinking a stranger broke into my room. Oh, and I read maybe one a day, or a few each week. It depends on the length of the book. You should read these as well."

I chuckle. "You want me to read a romance novel? That sounds like something a girl would do. Give me a manly book with blood and gore, and I'll bury myself in those pages." I don't want to let on that I love a good romance novel myself now and then. Okay, maybe I actually read them often.

She looks up at me and flashes me a dazzling smile. "I wonder where it is then... where you learn your romantic tendencies from. Reading romance novels could be very informative to guys. You could learn a thing or two from the male leads."

"My romantic side is natural, baby. I was born this way. A book can't teach me anything I don't already know," I say as I lick my lips and rub my hands suggestively.

She throws her head back and laughs. The sound is as beautiful as the music of angels.

"So what is this?" She mimics the action of rubbing her hands and licking her lips.

"That's swag, my love."

"Swag? Who told you that girls find that romantic? You look like a thirsty mosquito or a praying mantis."

I pout playfully at her. "Ouch! That hurts." I clasp at my chest.

"I'm sorry, but it's true. Men think wiggling their eyebrows at us or doing what you were doing is sexy, but really, it isn't, especially when you're dressed like that."

I shrug and slump on the bed next to her. "I just thought it was romantic, you know?"

She leans over to the side of the bed and pulls out a romance book from under the pillow. "Use this. It's the best manual for what girls really like."

I take the book and study the cover. A man is kissing the neck of a woman whose blouse is slightly off her shoulder.

"Blah," I say and toss the book to the side. I actually think I've read it before.

"Continue being a praying mantis then," she says.

"No, I want to learn. I would rather you teach me, though. I don't want to know what those women in the stories want. I want to know what you want."

A pink shade creeps into her cheeks. "Are you sure you want to know what I want?"

I lean my weight on my elbow and prepare to take mental notes. "Of course. I want to know what the woman I love desires. Teach me, my love."

She cups my chin in her warm hands. "Assure me that you'll give me what I need without complaining. I really want this badly. If you can give it to me just how I want it, you can rub your hands and lick your lips all you want. I won't call you a hungry mosquito or praying mantis; I'll just look at you with admiring and loving eyes. So are you ready to give me what I want?"

I reach down to loosen the servant chinos I'm wearing. As she speaks, I can feel them tighten around my groin. It's either they are shrinking, or something inside them is growing bigger.

"I am ready to give you whatever you want and any way you want it, darlin'. Just say the word."

She looks deep into my eyes and leans in. I feel her sweet breath caressing my skin. I think she's going to kiss me, so I close my eyes.

"I want some pickles and peanut butter."

Damn! She had my mind racing there for a bit. Parts of me had woken up to those suggestions, yet I was way off.

"You are such a tease," I complain.

"I told you, the best manual," she raises the book she's reading in the air and waves it.

"I guess you're right," I answer. I will my mind to calm down the tension built in my pants. I think of Emily blowing me a kiss and winking, and the imagery works like a charm to deflate my manhood.

"Where are Shelby and Kelly? One of them could bring some for me," Rose suggests.

"They are out... running errands. On a scale of one to ten, how badly do you need to eat pickles and peanut butter right now?"

"A hundred," she responds without hesitating. Pregnancy cravings are indeed a thing.

"Okay. I'll have to go and get you the snack. I pray no one sees me. If they do, I hope they don't recognize me."

"I don't recognize you. I'm sure no one else will."

I nod and make my way out the door and toward the kitchen. My heart stops when I see Beta Adam making his way toward me. I look down at the ground and hope he pays me no mind. Although his wife knows the whole plan, I doubt he has been told.

As we pass each other, he stops.

"Hey, who are you? You're coming from Lady Rose's room. What were you doing in there? I've never seen you around here, and male servants don't have chamber duties." Beta Adam shouts. "Don't make me ask again."

I wonder if I should stop and answer or continue on my way. He takes quick steps after me and grabs my arm.

"Chill, man. It's me," I whisper.

He looks at me confused. "You, who?"

I roll my eyes. "Alpha Reece."

"You must think I'm stupid. I know Alpha Reece, and you, sir, or not him."

"Boom shakalaka laka?" I say desperately. I see the menacing look leaving his eyes.

"Alpha Reece? That's really you? What are you doing here? Why are you dressed like this?" Beta Adam's questions flew out one after another.

"Long story, but my cover can't be blown. I need to go grab pickles and peanut butter. Pregnancy things," I say quickly.

As we prepare to go to the kitchen, Emily comes rushing down the hallway.

"What is all this noise?" she asks.

She looks at me and dismisses me like I am invisible.

"I was just talking to this servant here," Beta Adam explains.

"Who the hell is he? Why is he moving around these parts of the palace? Male servants aren't allowed on this side unless they're fetching one of us for the king. What are you doing here? Are you a pervert? A peeping Tom? Speak, you dirty piece of filth," Emily demands as she looks at me.

I raise my head to look at her. My heart is racing, but her insult struck a nerve. Who was she calling filth? As my eyes fixate on her face, she spits into my eyes.

"Don't you dare look me in the eye, pervert! My cousin will hear about such insolence," she threatens and marches off.

"Damn, I'm sure she will bring the king. I forgot servants can't look the masters and madams in the eye. I was still in my Alpha element there. My bad. I need to leave."

We speed walk back to Rose's room.

"Darlin', Beta Adam will have to look after you. He will get you your peanut butter and pickles. I need to go now. I love you," I insist as I bend down to kiss her.

"But…" she stammers.

"Beta Adam will explain."

I hear footsteps coming down the hall. I jump out of the window and hold onto the ledge as I listen.

I can hear the booming voice of the king coming from Rose's room. "Where is he?"

"Who?" I hear Beta Adam ask.

"That perverted derelict servant you were standing with in the hallway." Emily's voice says firmly.

"I wasn't standing with anyone. I was here all this while just about to go and get Lady Rose her snack," Beta Adam says defensively.

"You are a liar. I saw you with a weird-looking servant in the hallway. He even had the nerve to look me in my eyes, and I spit in his face."

"Miss Emily, I think all the sex you had with Alpha Stephen last night messed with your head. I was not in the hallway, and there was no strange servant. Alpha Stephen left in such a hurry today saying the spanking games you demanded from him got a bit too wild. Are you sure you didn't get a knock on your head during the whole wild sex thing?"

I can hear the king clearing his throat noisily. I stifle a laugh. Purity myth busted!

When I hear footsteps move away and Emily's loud voice fading as she insists, "It's not what you think cousin," I climb down and quickly shift into my wolf form, making pace to try to catch up with the other Alphas.

CHAPTER 24: FIGHTING ALPHA KANE

MARK

Dusk settles over the front line of our defenses, and in the distance, we can sense the enemy standing amongst the trees in the forest. All of us are in our wolf forms now. All of us are ready to attack. We're just waiting for the sky to transform itself fully into night so that we can operate under the cover of darkness.

It's what wolves do best.

Thankfully, since we are all Alphas, I can mind-link with the others in my party that I am sure are equally as worried about Rose. Having left her there in the castle with Reece, I am not quite as concerned as I would be if she were completely alone, but still, something inside of me says this won't be good, and we are not as close to the castle as I would like to be.

Though, I am also glad that the battle is unfolding several miles away from where Rose and our babies are staying. If the battle were any closer, I wouldn't be able to concentrate on the enemy. I'd be too busy looking behind me to make sure she's safe.

"It won't be long now," Tristan says from his position to my right. He has his best warriors with him, as do I. Eli is far to the left of me, and Reece's men are in between us. They are under the command of his Beta, Wessley, though none of them know why. They didn't question their Alpha's thinking, though. They just prepared for battle as they always did.

"It won't be long," I agree with Tristan, and I am ready for this fight. I am ready to rip into Alpha Kane's forces, to tear their throats out with my very teeth. How dare he think that he can come in here and threaten the woman I love?

With the fall of night, we begin to creep forward through the woods. I stay in front of my men, not sure what we will see when we come into contact with Alpha Kane and his warriors, but I'm sure the other Alpha has his own network of allies standing against us.

It won't be easy.

As I lead my warriors through the woods, I glance over and see a familiar wolf commanding the troops to my left, and I freeze for a moment.

What the hell is Reece doing here?

I catch his eye, and his wolf sort of shrugs.

"Why are you here?" I ask him. "What about Rose?"

"Well, we had an issue," he explains. "Don't worry. Beta Adam is taking care of her." He is using the mind-link to explain to all of us Alphas at once.

"But… is she safe?" I ask him.

"Yes, yes. Adam, Kelly, and Shelby won't let anything happen to her. Emily saw me and had the king coming to check on me. Thankfully, I got away in time. I couldn't risk him recognizing me." His explanation doesn't quite answer all of my questions, but a fierce howl pierces through the night as every wolf in front of us seems to join in the haunting melody.

All of a sudden, we are under attack.

I don't stand by and wait for Alpha Kane's wolves to close in on me. Instead, I give the command for my warriors to surge forward and meet them as they come over a slight rise in the ground in front of us. We trample the forest floor, moving quickly, and then, we collide with the enemy in a thunderous boom that rocks the forest around us.

I make short work of the first son of a bitch I tangle with, flipping him over onto his back and ripping his jugular from his neck like he's nothing more than a newborn pup. Then, I move on to another and another.

By the time I reach my fourth wolf, blood coats my tongue and teeth. I can taste the metallic, sticky substance all the way down the back of my throat. Little tufts of fur are embedded into it, and normally that would make me choke a bit, but I'm still after the enemy, and I'm not about to let a few bites of the vanquished slow me down.

I move forward, and in the distance, I see him…. A large silver, gray wolf with blood dripping from his canines as he prowls through the woods, looking for another enemy to tear apart.

"Kane," I say to myself as my gums curl back in a sneer. A low growl emits from the back of my throat, and immediately, my paws carry me toward him. I dodge around other wolves who would like to have a piece of me, but they aren't fast enough, and soon, I find myself staring right into Kane's eyes.

"Well, if it isn't Alpha Mark," he says, glaring right back at me. "We meet again."

"I'm going to rip your head off, you asshole," I tell him, bending at the knee so that I can launch my attack.

"I'd like to see you try, you pathetic fuuu—"

He doesn't get the rest of his sentence out as a large dark wolf plows into him from the right, knocking him against a tree, hard with a lot of force behind it.

"What the hell?" I ask, trying to figure out what's happened.

Then I recognize the wolf, and it all becomes clear.

"Tristan!"

Before Tristan can explain himself, a bunch of other wolves from Kane's side are upon us, here to defend their leader. They knock Tristan backward, six of them against only one of him, which gives Kane a chance to stumble to his feet.

I want to get at him, to finish what I've started, but now there are several of his wolves on me, and I have to fight them off just to stay alive.

It's not as difficult as it might seem, though there are five of them and only one of me, but they aren't as fast, and their fighting skills aren't as prominent either. I grab the smallest one by the neck and use him as a club to knock the others down. Then, I rip his throat out and move on to the next one as he's starting to get up. As I tear into the third, my men catch up with me from behind, and that spooks the final two into running away.

"Well, that didn't go as planned," Tristan remarks through the mind-link, shaking his head. His shoulder is bleeding a little, but he's taken out all of Kane's men that attacked him.

"Why the hell did you interrupt me?" I ask, stomping over to him. It seems clear now that Kane's men are losing severely, and as wave after wave of our warriors rush around us, chasing them down, I can't help but question my Alpha friend.

"What do you mean? I was giving him the ol' one-two."

"The ol' one-two?" I question, having no idea what the fuck he's talking about–as usual.

"Yeah, you distract him–that's one. And I come in and rip his head off. That's two," he replies.

I shake my head at him. "That was not what I had in mind," I tell him. "And it didn't work."

"Well, let's go get him and give him the ol' one, two, three," Tristan suggests.

I don't bother to ask what that is.

As the two of us start to run forward, I hear Eli's voice in my head, and he's frantic. Tristan stops short as well, and I know Eli is talking to both of us.

"Guys! We have to get back to the castle right away!" Eli is shouting. "It's Rose!"

My heart leaps into my chest, and I feel all of the blood leaving my head. I can no longer think straight as my heart races and my breathing becomes shallow. "What is it?" I ask, turning around to head to where I last saw Eli on the battlefield. Tristan comes with me. The battle is tilting so far in our favor now, we don't need to worry about Kane. I send a message to my Beta to keep pushing Kane's forces back.

"I don't know exactly," Eli says as his red wolf comes into view ahead of me. "But Kelly just said to hurry back. Emily is up to something. She knows that we're all gone."

"Did she try to hurt Rose?" Reece asks as he appears from behind a pine tree on my right.

Eli is quiet for a moment, and I assume he's talking to his sister. When he looks up at us, his eyes are wide. "Oh, Goddess. It's… Morris!"

"Morris?" I repeat. "But we ran him off. He went home."

"Does that little bitch seriously want my magic wand up his ass that bad that he came back?" Tristan growls.

"I don't know," Eli admits. "Kelly just said Morris is there. Something about a knife!"

That's all I need to hear. I turn around and run back toward the castle as fast as I can go, knowing the other Alphas are on my heels.

I don't care about the war. I don't care about being the next king. I don't care about anything else in the world except for Rose and our babies.

If anything ever happens to any of them… there will be hell to pay.

CHAPTER 25: MORRIS IS A MORON

Tristan

The volcanic rage surging in me is distracting me from the pain in my shoulder. I have no time to listen to anyone explain what has happened. Morris has been warned, but he has the guts to call our admonitions a bluff.

A group of our warriors is right on our heels as we arrive, and we all quickly throw on some pants.

"Where is he?" I bark as I push through the war room doors, followed closely behind by the other three Alphas. I can hear from their heavy breathing and hushed curses that they're just as pumped up to lay their hands on Morris as I am.

"What are you all doing back here?" King Gene asks as he jumps to his feet.

"Where is Morris?" I repeat my question, not bothering to give him an answer.

"He's shackled in the crypt," Beta Adam offers.

I nod my thanks, and the four of us storm out of the room, heading toward the dungeons.

"Tristan, do you know where the crypt is?" Mark whispers to me.

I curse silently as the other three men look at me expectedly. We

BELLA MOONDRAGON & OLIVIA BHELLE KILDARE

had made quite the dramatic entrance and exit, but now I had to go back in there, undoing our perfect theatrics.

"Sorry, but where is the crypt?" I ask, standing back at the door.

"I'll show you," Beta Adam responds as he makes his way to us. The slight tilt of his mouth makes me think he wants to laugh at how my voice has shifted from a booming angry speech to a polite inquiring tone.

He walks in front of us toward some stairs at the end of the south wing. The stairs go down to what I assume is a crypt, basement, or dungeon of some sort.

"It's a great thing I was there. Alpha Morris busted into Lady Rose's room without even knocking. Someone must have shown him exactly where her room was. I was in the bathroom and peered through the crack opening of the door to see him take out a fisherman's knife from his belt and begin swinging it about. Lady Rose screamed to alert me about the intruder, but I had already seen him and pounced on the bastard."

"So, Emily isn't giving up, is she? I thought Alpha Stephen would have spanked the obsession with Rose out of her," I say.

"I doubt she will ever give up. Even with Alpha Stephen warming up her inner thighs, she's still determined," Reece adds.

"Maybe the old man is as ice cold as his stone heart and attitude, so he's failing to warm her up effectively," Eli reasons.

"Is Rose okay?" Mark asks.

"Alpha Morris didn't touch her. She's shaken, but all right. Shelby and Kelly are with her now. They had already discussed possible sleeping arrangements to make sure that she's never left alone. I think I heard them discuss bathroom schedules too," Beta Adam explains.

I raise a brow. "Bathroom schedules?"

"Yes. They think it best to guard her around the clock. That means they will also guard her in the bathroom."

"That's a bit too much. I doubt she would want to take a dump while someone watches," I argue.

Eli chuckles. "Women go to the bathroom in groups, so I doubt that it's weird. I mean they already do that thing of showing each other their butt cracks... I thought you knew a lot about women. It seems I know something you didn't know then."

We all stop and turn to glare at Eli.

"Sorry, I stopped listening at butt crack. Is that what you said or am I hearing things?" Reece asks, a look of pure shock on his face.

Eli looks at all of us and answers, "You mean y'all don't know that women show each other their butt cracks? Y'all have a lot to learn. Ask any woman, they'll tell you."

"Who told you this?" I inquire. I try my best to keep down the laughter bubbling in my chest.

"Kelly told me. Rose confirmed it," he answers with an air of pride.

"I think your sister was messing with you, buddy. Women don't show each other their butt cracks. Scratch that, nobody shows anyone their butt crack. Unless you have a weird rash after accidentally slipping and falling into a poison ivy bush naked with a pretty girl on top of you... then you need the doctor to take a look at it," I say.

This time they all turn to stare at me, puzzled.

I shrug. "Naked accidents happened a lot when I was younger. Sue me."

They all shake their heads, and we continue down the stairs.

When we get to the crypt, I immediately hate the place. It smells of urine and old people, but the bastard who tried to kill our Rose is here, so I push down the nauseated feeling as I try to adjust my eyes to the dim lighting.

Alpha Morris is shackled in one corner of the room. His lanky frame is unmistakably shaking like a leaf in a strong April wind.

"I will kill you!" Mark shouts, but Eli holds him back before he can advance toward the coward.

Alpha Morris cowers back into the wall behind him. "I—"

"Shh. Don't say a thing," I warn as I shake my fist. My heart is pounding as the suppressed rage comes back, cocked and loaded. I bully my way closer to him, and I'm afraid he will melt into the wall he's now flattened against. He's so skinny, and his crouched pasty form seems to be blending well with the gray wall he hopes will protect him.

I crouch in front of him and inch my face toward his. "Look at me, fool," I order.

He raises his pallid face until our eyes connect. He looks like he has been crying. His tear-stained cheeks confirm my suspicions while his pale, boney, spotted hands tremble.

I can feel the presence of the other Alphas and Beta Adam standing behind me. Their rage isn't too hard to miss as it poisons the atmosphere and would make anyone pray for a quick death.

"Do you have all your affairs in order, buddy?" I ask.

His look turns from terrified to confused. He nods and shakes his head simultaneously.

"My fellow Alpha there told you what would happen if you ever attempted anything so stupid, right? Did you assume he was joking? You surely must have a death wish for you to defy us," I say in a controlled low voice punctuated with anger.

"M... Miss Em... Emily said you weren't there. She promised to take my virginity and pay me a lot of money if I came down and did as she wished," he stutters.

"So, you would kill our woman and our children for a little taste of Emily's bitter, slimy intimate juices?" I ask.

He blinks up at me; he doesn't seem to understand what I'm referring to.

"I just want to be a real man," he whimpers.

"Real men don't stab helpless women, idiot. Real men protect the weak. Real men find real women to give their virginity to, not whores."

He swallows. "I'm in my thirties and have never seen a woman naked," he confesses as a tear rolls down his face.

"Emily was never going to show you her naked body. She wasn't going to sleep with you either," Reece's voice comes from behind me.

I nod. "Do you think Emily would sleep with you? Have you met yourself? And what the hell is that smell?" I pinch the bridge of my nose.

Morris's face turns even more ash white. "I was so scared, and I needed to use the toilet. When I'm scared, my bowels get loose. I'm sorry."

I scrunch up my nose. "You mean you shit yourself?"

He nods and more tears roll down his cheeks.

"Gentleman, this man isn't worth our rage. He's punishing himself already," Mark observes as he too pinches his nose.

"Listen, Morris. Rose is our woman. We are four of the most feared and strongest Alphas around. Your type doesn't want to mess with us, our woman, or our children. Or else, if you do, your death will be painful. Actually, if you had succeeded in so much as cutting the ends of her hair today, your whole pack would pay for every strand of that hair with a life, a life for every strand of hair. Do you understand me?" I ask.

He nods feverishly. "So, will you push your magic wand up my ass?"

I smirk. "I have a better plan for you, Morris." I ruffle his hair and get up.

After telling the other men to wait for me, I ran up to my room. When I return, I find Eli giving Morris a lecture.

"Emily sent her chambermaid to kill Rose. She failed, but guess what happened to her. She's in a dingy dungeon awaiting her day to be hung. Guess what happened to the person who sent her? She's up there getting other idiots like you to do her bidding and take the fall. Don't be that foolish. Your pack might be small, but the least you can do to stand out would be using some intelligence and having some integrity."

I smile as I walk toward them. The smell seems even more pungent now.

I throw the doll that I'm holding at him.

"Wh… what is this?" Morris asks.

"That's Luna Lula. She is a blow-up sex doll. She'll help you practice your sexual advances. If you want to ask nicely, she might even take your virginity. Just treat her well, and please go find yourself a real woman. If we're satisfied that you're living a good life, and doing your best to keep your pack on an ethical path, we'll call on you to form alliances with us from time to time. Being on great terms with any of our packs is worth more than what Emily can offer you," I explain honestly.

"Also, I heard your pack has highly skilled blacksmiths. Maybe if you stop being greedy, we could offer you a contract to design tools and equipment for us and market your skills to other packs on your behalf. That would help with your debt," Mark reminds him.

Morris wipes his face with the back of his hand and nods. "Will you really do that for my pack?"

I smile. "Of course, Morris. Just remember, terms and conditions apply."

CHAPTER 26: THAT WASN'T HARD

GENE

I can't help but pace back and forth through my office. The Alphas have gone down to the crypt to speak to Alpha Morris. Only my Beta remains in my office. I want some answers, but I don't even know where to begin.

"Where did those asshole Alphas go to?" I demand from Adam, even though I know the answer.

"They went down to address Alpha Morris," he replies, calmly. He is leaning against the wall, his hands folded in front of his stomach.

"And how is the war going?" I ask, wishing I could be out there battling. But then… I've never been as powerful on the battlefield as I am in my office in the castle.

"We have won the day," Adam assures me. "The Alphas secured the battlefield before they came back to the castle. Their Betas are taking care of things now, taking prisoners and what have you."

"Good, good," I reply under my breath. "And Kane?"

Adam clears his throat, and I don't know what that means at first, but then I realize it's bad news.

"The fucker got away?" I ask him, and he nods.

"Yes, he escaped, but I'm sure we will catch him."

I can't help but slam my fist into the palm of my other hand. "Damn it!" I shout. "Those fuckers should've never left the battlefield when he was still alive!"

"In all fairness, Your Majesty," Adam begins, "they came back because their children were in danger. You must understand that, Sir. You sent Alpha Morris to the crypt as soon as you realized he'd tried to kill your heirs."

I don't know what to say to that. I did send Alpha Morris down to the dungeon as soon as I realized what he was up to, but I wasn't in the middle of a battle either. Besides, I really had no choice. I wish the bastard would've been quicker with his knife or Adam wouldn't have stopped him. That would've solved a big problem for me.

A few moments later, I hear heavy footsteps in the hallway, and I know that the Alphas are back. The four of them pour into my office, all of them looking irritated. I don't blame them. I am irritated. "Why the fuck did you guys leave the battlefield without taking Kane's head?"

Mark scows at me. "I almost had him, but he ran off. Don't worry about Alpha Kane, Your Majesty. We will get him. We need to deal with the murderer in the castle first."

I scoff at him, but then, I admit, "Yes, that's a good idea. What are we going to do with Alpha Morris?"

"Morris?" Tristan says. "We aren't talking about Alpha Morris, Sir," Tristan clarifies. "He's not the murderer."

"What do you mean?" I demand. "He's the one that Beta Adam caught with the knife!"

"Yes, he is the one that was caught with the knife," Alpha Reece clarifies. "But he's not the one behind it. That was your cousin, Emily, again."

"And we are getting fucking tired of her bullshit," Tristan adds.

"Excuse me?" I demand, not happy about his attitude. "Listen, I am the king, and she is my cousin!"

"She is a murderer, responsible for killing the chef," Alpha Eli says, "and she is the one who has tried to kill Rose multiple times. We are done playing around, King Gene. We mean you no respect, but we're not going to sit around and wait for you to do something about Emily. We are the ones that were just out there fighting to protect your castle, your subjects, and your position as king. But I don't remember seeing you out there bleeding, sweating, working your ass off for anything."

"How dare you!" I exclaim. "I am YOUR king, YOUR sovereign!" Did he misspeak or did he mean to say he doesn't respect me?

"And we are done protecting you if you don't get that bitch out of this castle right now!" Tristan shouts at me.

I am stunned. I have no idea how to respond to that. I can't even form a sentence. I can't remember the last time anyone spoke to me that way. My mouth is open, but I am sputtering.

"Close your mouth, Sir," Reece demands. I am shocked by his order. An Alpha ordering me, the king?! He continues before I can scold him. "Close your mouth, and listen. Emily is done. She can marry Alpha Stephen. We will figure out who the Luna is later, but that's the least of your problems. If you don't do this, you're going to have to fight us."

"All of us," Tristan chimes in, and I can't help but glare at all of them and gulp at the thought of combat with these muscular maniacs.

"Do it," Mark says. "Just do it. Send the bitch out of here before someone else gets killed."

"Are you threatening my life?" I ask Mark.

He shakes his head, but Tristan adds, "I am telling you that we will fight you. We will bring all of our warriors against you, if you don't get rid of that fucking bitch right now!"

I am still stunned, but I feel my head rocking back and forth as I agree, "Fine. I will call him. I will ask Alpha Stephen to come back to the castle so that I can see if he is willing to take Emily."

I disagree with the strong-arm tactics that the four Alphas are approaching me with. I am not used to being told what to do, and I have a long memory. I will hold it against them. I will find a way to make sure all four of these Alphas pay for their behavior today.

But right now, with their forces outside of my castle, ready to turn on me, I have little choice. "I'll call him, and I'll send Emily away. But don't think that this means that that disgusting Breeder is going to be the next Luna of my kingdom. That will never, ever happen!" I insist firmly.

I can tell by their expressions that they don't want to talk about that at this moment.

Tristan folds his bulging arms across his chest. "That's fine. Let's just nip this in the butt."

"Nip it in the... butt?" Mark repeats, looking at him strangely.

"Yeah, get it over with already," Tristan clarifies.

"Uhm, first of all, that's not what that means. It means to get it over with quickly, and this has been dragged out forever. And then... it's bud. Not butt."

"No, I'm pretty sure it's butt," Tristan counters.

"No, it's not. It's bud," Mark insists.

I sigh. "Who the fuck cares? Get out of my office so I can call Alpha Stephen and get his flaccid old ass back here!"

"Let's go check on Rose," I hear Alpha Eli say, and he is pulling on Alpha Tristan's arm. I am glad they are getting ready to go. I need some quiet in this office so I can think.

The Alphas leave my office, and I hear one of them, Alpha Reece, I think, say, "That was too easy," and I think he's right.

It was too easy, and I'm not convinced that I'm actually going to do what they want me to do. But I will call Alpha Stephen and get his wrinkly ass back here so I can decide what to do with him.

I agree, Emily is a menace. She is a problem. This is definitely not working out the way that I expected it to.

I go back to my desk and see that Adam is still there. "You can go, too," I demand. "I am disappointed in you, Beta Adam," I say as he walks toward the door. He freezes in his tracks and turns to look at me. "You were supposed to be able to handle this. The woman was supposed to die, but not until those babies were out of her." At this point, I don't care when it happens. It just needs to happen.

He clears his throat. "I'm sorry, Your Majesty," he apologizes, but I can tell by the look in his eyes that he doesn't mean it.

Perhaps he is not as loyal as I have always assumed he is.

Waving him away, I pick up my phone and dial Alpha Stephen's number. I wait for his secretary to patch me through. "Alpha Stephen," I say. "It's King Gene. I need you to come back to the castle tomorrow."

"Yes, of course, Sir," he agrees. He hasn't been gone too long. He stayed the entire night after her ball. I believe he was spending a lot of time with Emily. I walked past her room a few times, and it sounded like they were having tickle fights.

I love a good tickle fight....

"May I ask what this is regarding, King Gene?" the Alpha asks.

"It's in regards to my cousin, Emily," I inform him. "I feel that the two of you may have made a good match, and I would like to discuss the possibility of the two of you being joined in wedded bliss."

Alpha Stephen clears his throat and says, "One moment, please." Then, he lowers the phone, thinking that it works the same as pressing mute, but I can still hear his ignorant ass as he yells, "Yes! Yes! Yes! I'm going to be king!"

I roll my eyes and wait. When he lifts the phone, I clarify, "No, this does not mean that you will be the next king. I simply need my cousin out of the castle–for now. She's causing more harm than good, and she's angered the other four Alphas that are in line for the throne."

"Oh." I hear the disappointment in his voice. "That's... fine, Sir.'

"Just be here tomorrow morning," I instruct him. "We can speak more about it then. But... you do want to marry her, don't you?"

"Of course," he says eagerly, and I think that this is the best way to go, regardless of what it means for the situation with the Breeder and the four Alphas. I haven't met many people willing to marry my cousin, even with the possibility of the throne as the grand prize. She's too troublesome for her own good.

I hang up the phone and take a deep breath. The Alphas think that this has been too easy, and they are right.

Because it isn't over yet.

CHAPTER 27: THE FATE OF THE NEXT LUNA

Emily

I am so gorgeous... none of those stupid fucking Alphas even deserve me. Yet, they think they want that stupid Breeder bitch instead. They must have been brainwashed from that bitch herself.

I stare at my reflection in the mirror, brushing out my long, dark hair, waiting to hear from the pack healer, Dr. Penderghastly, that the Breeder and her babies are all dead. Surely, she will make some sort of an announcement soon.

I wonder if cousin Gene has an intercom here. If he does, he's never used it, but I can imagine the doctor coming over the PA system and saying, "Excuse me, everyone, may I have your attention please? I'm here to tell you that the big nosed Breeder with the giant stomach is dead. Since no one likes her anyway, we will just dump her body in the lagoon out behind the castle where all of the wastewater goes. She will be floating with shit. Now, go on about your business."

I laugh to myself, and when my new maid, I-Don't-Fucking-Give-A-Shit-What-Her-Name-Is, or Idfgaswhni for short, gives me a strange look. I glare at her. She cowers immediately, ducking her head.

A hard knock on my door has me startled at first, but then

delighted, as I imagine that I'm finally going to be getting the news that Alpha Morris's murderous task from yesterday was carried out successfully, and sadly–although surely nobody will be shedding tears–the bitch is dead.

"Well, don't just stand there, Ida," I demand to the maid, because that's easier than Idfgaswhni, "get the Goddessdamn door!"

She hops over to open it, and I see that worthless Beta, Adam, standing there. I roll my eyes. I doubt they'd send him to tell me that, after lingering all night in the infirmary, the bitch Breeder has died due to her stab wounds. "Yeah?" I say, not even looking at him.

"Your cousin would like to speak to you in his office. Now," he says, glaring at me, like he thinks I've done something wrong.

As he starts to walk away, I ask, "About what? Emily doesn't just hop up and run because someone tells her to."

"Even if it's the king?" he asks with much irritation in his voice. I shrug my shoulders and continue to run my brush through my hair. "Well, Emily needs to get her ass into the king's office before Adam puts his boot through it."

I stand, turning to face him. "How dare you speak to Emily that way! Don't you know who I am?"

"How dare you speak to Adam that way! Don't you know who I am?" he asks, his shoulders back and his chest pushed forward like a fucking peacock.

I roll my eyes again. "You're no one!"

"I am the Beta of this kingdom," he announces, looking into my eyes. "I am number two to the king!"

"So you're the king's shit?" I ask him, and I can't help but laugh. He narrows his gaze. "I'm going, asshole, but not because you told me to. Emily doesn't do what anyone tells her to do."

"Emily needs to grow up and stop referring to herself in the third person like a moron," Adam says as he follows me down the hallway to King Gene's office. I want to turn around and slap his face, but I just keep walking.

"Oh, there you are," King Gene greets me rudely from behind his desk. I swear that piece of furniture gets bigger every time I'm here. "What took you so damn long?"

"Your stupid Beta wanted to give me his life story on the way," I tell him as the Beta in question slams the door behind me. I sink down into a chair. "What is this about? Is it the Breeder? Is she dead?"

His face doesn't change as he looks at me for a long moment. "No," he finally replies. "You have to stop trying to kill people, Emily."

I moan. "I didn't do it," I assure him. "Besides… sometimes people need to be killed."

"Not her!" he yells with an emphatic tone. "Not yet! Now listen, your mischievous behavior has put me in a bad position with these four powerful Alphas. They've made threats against me, and now, well, I only have one thing left to do to appease them, and while I'm sure you aren't going to like it, I've already agreed to it."

My stomach sinks down all the way into my designer shoes. "What the fuck did you do?" I demand.

His eyes widen. "Don't you take that tone with me, you little bitch! I'm the king!"

I say nothing, but I feel tears stinging my eyes. Emily is losing, and Emily doesn't like that.

"You are going to marry Alpha Stephen. He's here to collect you."

King Gene's words seem definitive, like there's nothing I can say to change his mind, and that makes me want to hurl the stapler off of his desk at his head. "What?" I ask, still in shock.

"That's right. It's the only way I can keep the Alphas from rising up against me." He folds his arms across his measly little chest.

I shake my head. "No. I won't do it. Alpha Stephen is older than my grandfather, our grandfather, and his dick is as limp as a biscuit just put into the rising drawer. No. You can't make me."

"I can make you," he threatens, leaning forward and glaring at me. "And I will make you. And I don't want to hear another word about your sexual misconduct, Emily! I thought you were a pure, virginal woman who would make an excellent Luna, and it turns out you have more stickers on your ass than Phileas Fogg's suitcase!"

"Who the fuck is Phileas Fogg?" I ask, but he just shakes his head.

I figure he's probably some friend of the king's I haven't met yet. Another short, incompetent old man. Just like my soon-to-be husband.

"But Gene!" I exclaim.

"That's King Gene to you, young lady," he corrects. "There's nothing you can do about this, Emily! It's done. Now, if it makes you feel any better, the Beta of Alpha Stephen's pack is a nice, strapping young gentleman. Perhaps you can find some solace in his embrace?"

I stare at him for a moment, one eyebrow raised. "Do you have a photograph?"

He grumbles under his breath and reaches into a bottom drawer of his desk. A moment later, he pulls out a spiral-bound book that looks like something a kindergarten teacher would put together for a class project. On the cover, it reads, "Who's Who in the Kingdom: A King's Guide to Remembering People's Names." It's laminated....

He opens it up, flips through a few pages, and slides it across the desk to me.

Instantly, my eyes bulge. "Wow! He looks exactly like Alpha Reece!" My eyes drop down the page a bit, and I realize that's because the picture is of Alpha Reece. Under the photo, it says, "Alpha Reece" and has his pack name.

"Son of a bitch," King Gene mutters and flips the page again. "Here."

This time, I am faced with a man who is nearly as good-looking as Alpha Reece. It says, "Beta Barnabas," under his picture.

"Barnabas?" I repeat.

King Gene shrugs. "So what? He goes by Barney."

I almost laugh. What a ridiculous name. "Is he a big purple dinosaur? Is he a bumbling deputy in a small town?"

"What the fuck are you talking about?" King Gene asks me, and I feel better about his Phony Flogg comment earlier, or whatever the hell he said.

"Fine," I huff with a sigh, knowing there's nothing else I can do to persuade him. I assume something has happened to Alpha Morris since he didn't kill the Breeder. He must've gotten caught. I don't want to take the fall for that.

"Great," King Gene says, sliding his book into the bottom drawer of his desk. He stands and walks me to the door, and when it opens, I expect to see Beta Adam there, but instead, it's Alpha Stephen.

"Already?" I ask.

"Well, you should go pack your bags," King Gene declares.

I groan under my breath. "That'll take ages."

"You have maids for that, I believe," he says. "Ones you haven't made murder anyone yet...."

I don't acknowledge anything. I just head back to my room, Alpha Stephen behind me.

Once there, I command the maids to start packing my bags, and I stand back, thinking about what this means.

Will I never be queen now?

"Say," Alpha Stephen begins, placing a hand on my back. "I thought... on the way home... we could...." He winks at me and makes a snapping sound between his cheek and teeth.

My stomach rolls over. "I don't think so," I tell him.

"Come on! I already took my medicine." He laughs and pulls me close enough to him that I can smell his sour mayonnaise breath.

This is going to be a long ride home....

"Take your time, Ida," I instruct. "Don't wrinkle my gowns."

She looks over at me and smiles before she shoves one of my expensive dresses into a suitcase, ignoring every word I say.

CHAPTER 28: ATTACKED WITHOUT WARNING

Eli

I shove my hands into the pockets of my jeans but then pull them out again. What is taking the other three Alphas so long to get here?

"Calm down, brother. I'm sure we will come up with a solution soon. Just breathe," Kelly tells me.

I inhale and exhale, but the relaxation technique is doing nothing to calm my nerves. The three men need to get here already so that I can tell them what's going on. We need to deal with this–and fast.

Tristan walks in, followed by Reece and Mark.

"What's wrong with you? Did Kelly shove her nunchucks up your butt?" Tristan quizzes.

I shake my head as I try to put what I'm about to say in an order that makes sense. "A messenger came in this morning from Elm Pack. An attack was launched against them last night. Eight of their wolves were killed, and five were wounded badly."

Mark hisses, Tristan curses under his breath, and Reece punches the wall next to him.

"Who's behind the attack? Kane?" Tristan asks.

I exhale sharply and shake my head. "The old bastard Stephen is apparently behind the attack."

"Why would he want to attack Rose's home?" Mark asks.

"I would have thought he'd be too busy spanking Emily to be launching attacks on Rose's pack. Does Rose know?" Tristan inquires.

"Yes. She's worried sick. She had been crying and locked herself in the bathroom. Poor girl. She came here just to be a Breeder, and now her life, and her parents' lives, are all in danger. We don't even know if Alpha Howard and Luna Karen are still alive," Kelly explains.

"This is kind of bizarre. Do you think Emily sent Stephen to do her bidding?" Reece asks.

"Honestly, I can't put anything past that witch. Alpha Stephen has no reason to attack Elm Pack. However, Emily is very cunning and has every reason to destroy Rose. It seems she isn't relenting," I reason.

Running a hand through his hair, Reece suggests, "Maybe we should go and console Rose."

"No, mate. I think we need to console her in a more effective way. Actions speak louder than words. Alpha Kane is hiding and probably trying to reboot, so we can go to Rose's home and fight off Stephen. If Rose finds out we've gone to fight for her pack, her family, that would mean more than any whispered sweet nothings coming from any of us," Mark tells us.

"Will it be safe leaving Rose here alone?" Reece asks, worry etched in his voice.

"Emily isn't here anymore, so Rose is probably safe from her," I add.

"We are wasting time, Alphas. We need to start heading in that direction now." Mark is growing more impatient by the second.

"Wheels roll in ten," Tristan confirms as he heads for the door. He stops at the entryway and turns to look back at Kelly. "Take care of her while we are gone. Don't leave her side," he pleads.

Kelly nods and turns to me. "Be careful, brother." She gives me a tight hug, and once she's released me, I start scrambling around to pack what I'll need for the trip. Rose's hometown is too far to head over to on foot, even in our wolf forms. It would just tire us out and leave us vulnerable for the fight ahead.

When I finally walk out of the palace, Tristan's forest green Jeep is already parked in the driveway. All the other Alphas are already waiting.

"Do you think we should have told the king about this?" I ask.

Tristan looks at me and scowls. "Do you think he cares about the fate of the 'dirty Breeder's' home? Besides, he is not my keeper. If he's not shelling out the gas money, it ain't his business."

I nod as I toss my pack in the back of the car. Tristan's right; the king will just try to talk us out of this mission. Alpha Stephen's attack wasn't directly impacting him or the palace, so chances are he wouldn't give a rat's ass.

Mark chimes in, "By the way, I caught how you told the king you meant no respect to him the other day."

"And he didn't even notice," I said, smiling.

He shook his head. "Anyway, I have a bunch of warriors riding behind us. They'll stay a little distance away; I'll call for them if we need back up," Mark affirms.

When threats are made directly or indirectly to someone I love, my defense mechanisms activate. Although I had never paid a visit to Elm Pack, I will treat their territory as if it was my own home and will guard it fiercely. What Rose treasures has now come to mean something to the four of us.

As the car heads down the road toward Rose's home, the journey is plagued with an awkward silence. We are all formulating our planned tactics in our heads.

"If you decide to do a one, two, five, or seven; please let me know in advance," Mark says sharply to Tristan.

I frown. "You want him to tell you when he is going to the bathroom? Y'all are becoming too close for comfort. I don't want to know anyone's bathroom schedule."

Tristan chuckles. "No, that's not what he's talking about. He means the ol' one-two. Someone distracts an attacker—that's one. And another one of us comes in and rips his head off. That's two."

I try to visualize what he's explaining and grin. "That sounds like a hell of a tag team. I would enjoy that innovative maneuver."

"Right? Tell that to grumpy Marky-Mark here," Tristan teases while steering the car to avoid a pothole in the road.

"Not that it's a bad move, but I just want you to warn me when we're doing it," Mark explains.

"Do any of you know where Rose's home is exactly?" Tristan asks.

I groan. "You mean you've been driving all this time not knowing the directions?"

Tristan shrugs. "I know the general direction, but not the exact GPS coordinates of her home. We're in the general area. I just need to find somewhere to stop and ask."

We all stare at him. We all blindly got into the car under the assumption that he knew where we were going.

He parks at a rest stop and climbs out of the vehicle. He's gone for a few minutes before he comes back with a plastic bag of snacks and drinks.

"Okay, so I know where it is now. We aren't that far actually," he clarifies.

I grab the bag and take out a package that looks like it contains beef jerky. I unwrap the packet and bite into the meat. I can really use some protein right now. The taste is off, causing me to spit it out immediately.

I look to my side and see Mark also spitting out the one he was attempting to eat.

"What the fuck is this nasty shit?" Reece asks.

Tristan smirks as he chews on his own piece with so much zeal. "Vegetarian jerky," he says proudly.

"Why would you buy vegetarian jerky? Also, when did you become a vegetarian?" Mark demands.

"First of all, I didn't buy it. The nice lady at the counter offered it to me for free. Second of all, I'm about to be a dad, and I know how it feels to have one's child under attack. I will not eat a poor cow's young one. Would you like it if someone ate your child?" Tristan asks. He steps on the gas, causing the car to lurch forward, and Mark's open drink splatters in his face.

Mark punches Tristan in the arm. "Drive like you've got some

THREATS AGAINST THE BREEDER

sense. Also, I doubt anyone would literally eat our children. We're wolf shifters. We need protein from real meat. How did you get so fucking huge without protein from meat?"

"Well, since finding out that I was going to be a father, I'm just trying to be more responsible. I want to create a better society for our children."

We are all silent as his words sink in. Tristan has a responsible side to him that seems to be hidden amongst the crazy pages of his life most of the time.

"That's good and all, but I prefer real meat," Reece argues.

Tristan throws his head back and laughs. "Yeah, me too. It was free, so I thought I'd give it a try, but it's like chewing on tree bark."

Ahh, this is the Tristan we all know and love. He veers the car to the side of the road and turns the engine off.

"Elm Pack is over that hill. We'll leave the car here and go there on foot. The car will make too much noise. We need to make sure our approach is silent."

After we shift, we move stealthily toward the hill. Tristan carries a bag in his mouth as we go for our clothes.

We slowly stalk through the last clump of trees that hide the entrance of Alpha Howard's homestead.

The house looks dark and abandoned. A window stands open, a torn white curtain billowing in the air as it's pulled in and out through the void.

Despite our heavily built frames, our movements remain fluid. We barely make a whisper as we put one paw in front of the other. I look at Reece, and he inclines his head at me. We're all quiet, as one who is stalking prey should be. My senses work tirelessly, as my sensitive ears take in every sound from the forest around us.

My ears perk up at every sound as we walk, whether it's a breeze whistling through the dense forest or the scamper of little animals looking for food. In direct contradiction to the pounding of my heart, my breath comes out in calm, controlled exhales. I can feel my heart beating in anticipation at the culmination of a long week of fighting off constant attacks lodged against us and the woman we hold dear.

The homestead is quiet… too quiet. I sniff the air. I don't smell the metallic stench of blood that usually lingers after a fight.

"Something is off," Mark interjects through the mind-link formed between all of us.

"Do you hear that?" I respond through the same link.

"No. It's too quiet," Tristan adds.

I shake my head as the hairs on the back of my neck stand on end. "Listen carefully. It sounds like it's coming from the forest around us. I think we walked into a trap."

The sounds increase in volume. I confirm, "I think it's an ambush!"

CHAPTER 29: REVENGE

T<small>RISTAN</small>

A swooshing sound in the air alerts me to the fact that something heavy is flying in my direction, before I even hear Reece's voice shouting in my head, "Watch out!"

I throw the bag toward a nearby rose bush and crouch down just in time to see a brown wolf tumble in front of me. I jump up, not giving him the time he needs to get up and regain his composure before I go for his neck. My teeth sink through the rough mane and into his jugular like a hot knife through butter; blood drips down the fur on my rostrum.

Looking around, I can hear snarling, the sound of pained howls and flesh tearing as they surround the place that was quiet moments ago.

To my right, Mark jumps and body slams his weight into a wolf making its way to Reece. Just as he does, I spot a black wolf jumping down at him from the roof of the abandoned house. How dare they try my ol' one-two on us. This maneuver is my invention, and I hold the copyrights to such brilliance.

I lean back, place my weight on my hind legs, and leap, bending my head slightly as my target comes into view mid-air. I meet the flying wolf with my charging frame, releasing the tension in my back, deliberately placing all my weight forward, and slamming into the attacking black wolf.

The wolf doesn't see me coming and flies into the wall of the house.

"Slam dunk!" I think as I land right in front of the wolf. He whimpers, trying to get back on his feet. "Tell your maker, Tristan says wassup!" I think as I tear out his throat.

A gray wolf comes charging at Eli from behind the house. "Time for the one ones," I say to him through the mind-link.

"What the heck is that?" he replies, a sound of agitation and confusion in his voice.

"Just tackle him. I'll do the second part," I reply.

As the wolf gets closer to Eli, he bends his forefeet slightly and does a speedy crawl and jump at the wolf's lower body. The crushing blow into its charging lower frame causes the wolf to tumble down. Before he can get up, I jump onto the wall, relying on the hard surface to give my hind feet a powerful spring. Leaning my weight to the side, I launch toward the wolf and pin him down with my paws.

I snarl and place my canines and incisors just at the base of his neck. I can see fear pass through the wolf's green eyes as he looks at me, waiting for me to finish him off....

I don't. Instead, I growl a warning causing the wolf to become still underneath me.

"We need him to tell us where Rose's parents are," I explain to Eli. "You need to shift."

"I'll be naked! Do you think I'll be as menacing if I interrogate him with my pecker hanging in his face?" Eli argues.

"The bag I had with me has some clothes," I remind him. "Go put them on while I hold this idiot down," I instruct, frustrated.

I continue snarling and baring my teeth at the wolf, although the fear in his eyes tells me he is done fighting.

"I don't think there are any more wolves around," Mark announces as he makes his way to where I still have the gray wolf trapped under me.

"Yeah," Reece agrees as he joins Mark.

Eli returns with the bag. The gray wolf has shifted into his human form. I guess it's a way to try to humanize himself to us and gain some type of sympathy so we don't kill him.

Eli takes the trembling, disheveled man and starts tying him up. We also get dressed in shorts, not bothering to put on shirts, and surround the bound man.

"Where are the occupants of this house?" Eli asks the man. He shrugs and then spits out some blood. My pounce must have caused more damage than I thought.

"Where are the Alpha and Luna of this household?" I rephrase the question. Again the man shrugs defiantly. Despite the fear written all over his face, this man is no Morris. He is still trying to hold on to the thin mirage of bravery he still has left.

Mark bends down and slaps the man across his face. "You will answer when asked!"

I laugh. "I think I need to bring out some of my tools to loosen our friend's tongue. I think I have just the thing to cure a case of 'cat got your tongue.'"

I rummage through my bag, knowing I really don't have any torture devices in there. My hand grasps something cold and I pull it out. I curse quietly when I realize all I have is one of those vegetarian beef jerky sticks. I'm not sure how I can use a stick of mashed vegetables as a torture device. Why had I even put this in the bag? What weird shit was I planning to use it for?

I shrug and turn back to the man, holding the vegetable jerky like a mysterious torture device. Maybe I could use it to poke out his intestines through his backside stinkhole.

The man takes a look at the jerky, and his eyebrows draw together. I pray he has no idea this is just a stick of vegetables.

"This, my friend, is a sweet-sweet torture device. If I shove it up your butt, you will chime like an ice-cream van before your honeyed death," I say. The other three look at me perplexed. What am I trying to say? Well, I hope he gets the point. This device could torture the truth out of him, if I use it correctly. I wonder if the bendy stick can even go up his stinkhole? It will be interesting to find out.

The man swallows hard as he looks at my 'torture device.' "They don't live here anymore. They moved up the cliff." We all look to where the man is pointing with his chin and see a huge mansion in the distance.

"Where is Alpha Stephen?" Mark asks.

The man looks at Mark and doesn't respond. I lift the stick and step toward him. He flinches.

"He's with other men up there. They will attack you as soon as you get there," he spills. I smile. Seems the vegetarian beef jerky has managed to get the truth from the fool.

Eli walks toward the rubble that's scattered around from the previous fight. He picks up a log and begins to inspect it.

"Before you think about taking up a new career as a carpenter, maybe we should go up there and rescue Rose's parents," I suggest.

Eli flashes a fake smile at me and walks toward the man. He lifts the hand with the log and crushes its weight against the guy's temple. The man falls to his side with blood flowing from the wound on his head.

"Okay, I guess the bastard is out cold," Reece observes.

"Or dead, who cares. Let's go," I say. We quickly shift back into our wolf forms and make our way up the cliff.

"What the hell did you bring that thing?" Eli asks through our mind-link.

"It worked didn't it?" I answer plainly.

"Genius! For a moment, I thought you might be pulling out one of your sex toys," Mark adds.

"I could figure out how to use it as such," I ponder.

"Tristan, Tristan," Mark laughs, shaking his head.

Before we even round the corner, we can make out the figures of our targets surrounding the mansion on top of the cliff.

They seem oblivious to our advancement. It proves fairly easy to fight through Stephen's wolf barriers.

"Head for the door. We'll join you shortly," Mark gives the order to me as he finishes fighting the last of the wolves surrounding the mansion.

The world begins to take on a red hue as my vision spreads out to the surrounding area, and through the trees. A huge gray wolf with brown speckles sees me coming toward the entrance of the mansion and stalks toward me. He's about seven feet high and four feet wide. His legs are wide as tree trunks, and he has menacing, poised claws on each of them.

He opens his slightly pointed maw and hisses while baring his numerous razor-sharp teeth at me. Stalking forward, he's in no rush, completely confident in his victory before the fight even begins.

"Fuck," I curse silently. What the hell is this monster?

I begin breathing rapidly as the blood courses through my body, preparing for a full-on fight. This wolf isn't going to be a pushover. I can feel a predatory howl fill my chest, and I let it loose. The other wolf emits a low growl and rushes toward me in a head-on charge. Even with the increased speed of my perception, the wolf's charge is a blur of movement.

I lunge forward as fast and focused as I can be. The wolf leaps at me, claws extended, and I jump to meet its charge. We collide midair, and the wolf's claws dig into my chest. I close my eyes and force my full weight into him, ignoring the pain.

"One-two," Mark's voice sounds in my head. I tumble underneath the wolf and swipe my forefoot at the wolf's hind feet; he loses his balance. Just as he does, Mark has the other wolf's neck in his mouth, tearing fur and flesh from it. The wolf's lifeless body slumps in a heap on my side.

I get up, nodding a thank you to my friend, and we all enter the house where Alpha Stephen should be.

Stephen is an Alpha, and it's not difficult to communicate with him using the mind-link.

He's standing between two chairs where a man and a woman are bound. I deduce that they're Rose's parents.

"Give up, Alpha Stephen. It's four against one," Reece tells him.

He has the same look the gray wolf at the old house had: fear and stubbornness.

"You might have won the battle, but the war is just beginning," he counters.

The four of us advance in his direction.

"Let's capture the bastard. We'll take him prisoner for this," Eli suggests.

We all agree and continue our advance. He takes a look at all of us, smirks, and jumps out through the window behind him.

Mark charges after him, but the selfish coward takes one of his wounded men in his mouth like a mother would a pup, and throws him at Mark. Mark catches the wolf in his mouth and tears at him in rage. By the time he's done, Alpha Stephen has disappeared into the forest.

"What if this was just a ploy to get us out of the palace? Emily might be attacking Rose as we speak," Reece suggests.

As we all dwell on the possibility, Eli clarifies, "I just spoke to Beta Adam. He says Rose is fine. Stephen's men and Emily are nowhere near the castle."

We all sigh in relief as we start trying to untie Alpha Howard and Luna Karen.

"Something still feels off," I muse to the other three.

CHAPTER 30: HER PARENTS ARE AWFUL

Mark

Once Alpha Stephen and his men are long gone, we are all dressed in our shorts again, so we untie Alpha Howard and Luna Karen. Eli has checked in with his sister back at the castle, and for the moment, everything seems okay. We need to take a run around the pack village here and make sure all is well, but I am curious to know the parents of the woman I love, and I assume the other Alphas are as well.

Luna Karen doesn't really look much like Rose. She has a really long, pointy nose, and her hair is a platinum blonde that looks like it came right out of a bottle. Alpha Howard doesn't look much like an Alpha to me. He is wiry with bug eyes that are a darker shade of the same color as Rose's, and his thinning hair is much darker than his daughter's.

I wonder how these two odd-looking people could be the parents of my beautiful Rose.

"So..." Tristan begins as the Luna and Alpha move to their sofa, both of them rubbing their wrists where the ropes have cut into their flesh. "You're Rose's parents?"

"Yes, that's right," Luna Karen affirms, rolling her eyes. "Maude? Are you still here? I need tea! I need it now!"

My head automatically inclines itself toward the kitchen. Are the servants still here?

"Bitch probably scrambled and hid when the commotion started," Alpha Howard says, shaking his head. "All of them are so fucking lazy."

"Can you imagine if Rose had been here?" Karen asks, and my ears perk up as I wait for her mother to say how strong and brave their daughter would be in the face of any danger.

"Goddess!" Alpha Howard exclaims, shaking his head further. "She would've peed her pants!"

"It would've been another mess, like when she worked at the sewage treatment plant," Luna Karen laughs.

I am shocked. My mouth drops open, and I turn to look at the other Alphas. They all look as surprised as I feel.

"You... think Rose wouldn't be courageous?" Reece asks for all of us.

"Are you kidding? That child is worthless! Almost as worthless as my maid. Maude! Maude!" Luna Karen shrieks again.

Tristan sighs and heads into the kitchen. I can tell by his expression that he is angry enough that he'll punch someone if he stays here.

"Rose isn't cowardly," Eli defends. "She's very brave. And smart. How can you speak of her that way?'

"Are you serious?" Rose's father asks. "Are you sure we're speaking of the same Rose? Rose Forest? Our daughter?"

"She's an awful mess," her mother adds, shaking her head. "And so... unattractive. It's a wonder that Alpha King Gene ever chose her to be the Breeder for those four Alphas."

Again, all we can do is stare at her. "We are those four Alphas," I finally announce. "We came here to help you because of Rose. Because we love her."

Luna Karen's eyes bulge, and Alpha Howard's mouth is so wide open, I can imagine a fly buzzing right in. "You... love her?" he asks me.

"More than anything," I reply. "We all do."

THREATS AGAINST THE BREEDER

Tristan strolls back into the room. "Well, I think I know why Maude isn't bringing the tea."

"Oh? Is she taking a nap again? That woman is useless. Useless, I tell you," Luna Karen says.

"No, she's not taking a nap. Not exactly. I mean... she is lying down." Tristan bites into his bottom lip, and I'm afraid he might draw blood.

"Well, get her up!" Alpha Howard insists. "The staff need to start putting the house back together."

"No one will be doing that except for maybe the Moon Goddess," Tristan explains. "Maude is dead."

"How do you know it's Maude that's dead?" Eli asks. "Couldn't it be another servant?"

"All of them are dead," Tristan explains. "They're all in the pantry in the kitchen, throats ripped out, in their human form. It looks like they never even had a chance to shift."

As I think about how awful Alpha Stephen and his men are, Luna Karen covers her mouth with both hands and begins to sob. "Oh, my!" she exclaims. "Oh, dear!"

I want to comfort her. She might've been rude to Rose, but she is her mother, so it's hard to see her so upset at the loss of her servants.. I take a step forward as Alpha Howard lifts a hand and puts it on his wife's shoulder. "There, there, darling. It'll be all right," he consoles her.

"But... we'll have to find all new staff! Who will make my tea?" Luna Karen asks, dabbing at her eyes.

"Your tea?" I repeat, baffled. She's crying because she has no one to serve her, not because her entire staff has been slaughtered–and it's all due to her own inability to providing proper protection.

"Yes!" she exclaims. "You see, we haven't been able to live this way for long. Before Rose was chosen, we had no staff. She had to do everything for us herself. Now, we have a staff and this lovely new house."

"Well, we did have a staff," Alpha Howard clarifies, shaking his head once more.

I can't help but hate these people at the moment. Are they completely heartless?

"You, big brooding Alpha with the dark curly hair," Luna Karen calls out, pointing at Tristan. "While you were in the kitchen, did you happen to see my tea kettle?"

Tristan looks like he wants to rip her head off. "I saw it."

"Perfect! Do you know how to make tea?" she asks, clasping her hands together excitedly.

"Uhm... I'm not going to make you tea. You haven't even thanked us for saving your life. You haven't asked one question about your daughter. What the hell is the matter with you?" He starts toward them, but Reece puts a hand on his chest to hold him back.

"Well, I'm sorry," Luna Karen says apathetically with a shrug. "I suppose I'm not thinking straight since I haven't had any tea for over an hour."

Before any of us can verbally lash out at her, Luna Karen's husband has the forethought to ask, "How is Rose? Is she truly pregnant?"

"She is," I tell him. "In fact, she's having four babies. You're about to be grandparents times four."

"Four babies?!" the Luna squeals and claps her hands together. "Oh, Howard! With four of them, at least one is bound to be a good one, unlike their mother."

"Yes, we can finally have the fruit of our loins accomplish something!" he adds, beaming.

"I don't think I like you very much," Tristan says with a snarl. "In fact, I kind of wish we would've let Stephen chomp your throats out."

Reece continues to hold him back. "I've never seen anyone so unappreciative of their child! Rose is amazing! She's smart, kind, and beautiful. Yet, you treat her like garbage. It's no wonder she never mentions that she misses you."

"How can you people live with yourselves?" Eli asks, the look of disgust on his face as obvious as Tristan's.

"Well... that's unfair," Alpha Howard states plainly. "You don't even know her, not like we do!"

"Oh, I beg to differ," I counter. "We know Rose very well. I told you, we love her. And our babies. And if the two of you continue to act like selfish spoiled assholes, I can guarantee you will never see a single one of those children."

Tristan adds, "If you don't get your shit in one sock, my baby is going to grow up thinking that his maternal grandparents are dead. And maybe they will be! We're not coming back here to protect you the next time Alpha Stephen attacks, so you best find yourself some money to pay for warriors and guards. Stop wasting Rose's hard-earned money on stuff like... this marble bust of a wolf's head!" He picks up what looks to be an expensive piece of art, and Luna Karen lets out a squeal.

"Put that down, Alpha!" she pleads. "That cost twenty thousand dollars!"

"You spent twenty thousand dollars on this piece of shit?" he asks.

I can feel both of the homeowners holding their breath as Tristan begins to juggle the item, tossing it up in the air and catching it–until he doesn't. It crashes onto the travertine floor and shatters into a million pieces.

"Oops," Tristan says, but I think he did it on purpose.

"How dare you!" Alpha Howard stands up and shouts, and his wife bursts into tears.

"What kind of people cry over a broken bust but not over their dead servants?" Eli asks.

"The kind that hasn't had their tea, apparently," Reece mutters.

"You'd better heed our words," I tell them. "Let's go."

I motion for the others to follow me, but we don't get too far before Eli stops us. "Can you believe those two bastards? We're the only family Rose has now. I can never see her coming back here."

"No, they're terrible people," Tristan agrees.

"It's not fair to the people who live in Rose's pack for us to leave them with those two assholes in charge when Alpha Stephen wants to attack again," Reece reminds us.

I sniff the air and know that Alpha Stephen is close by, and he's not alone. "You're right. We need to come up with a plan to keep the people in the village safe. Whatever happens to Rose's parents, I don't even give a shit, but those people deserve to be saved." I think of the slaughtered servants and wish we could've saved them instead of Rose's parents.

CHAPTER 31: ANOTHER THREAT

*Rose *

"All right, everything looks great," Dr. Pennygasket says as she helps me sit up. I am wearing one of those incredibly flattering hospital gowns that is wide open in the back with a sheet over my lap. She's pulled everything away from my protruding abdomen to check on my children. "I know the sexes now."

"Don't tell me," I say, covering my ears with both hands. "I don't want to find out without the Alphas." I'm not even sure where they are, but Shelby, Adam, and Kelly have all told me not to worry about it. They say that all four of my men are fine and just went to check on something in another pack.

I feel uneasy about the entire thing, but I am trying to go on about my day. At least this time, no one is in the doctor's office with me. I convinced both of my girlfriends to stay back in my room and wait for me there. I don't want an audience anymore while I'm at the doctor's unless it's my men.

"So just keep drinking a lot of water so that you stay hydrated, keep up your activity level for now, and try to get enough rest," Dr. Pentergastly tells me.

I nod. "All right, thank you, Doctor." I am glad I'll get to put my clothes back on soon. I really hate this hospital gown.

"You're sure you don't want to know what you're having?" Both the doctor and the nurse behind her have twinkles in their eyes.

"No, I want the daddies to find out at the same time as me," I tell her. I had seen all four of the babies on the little black and white plasma television when she was ultrasounding me, but I couldn't tell how many legs they had. I was just glad when she said they were all healthy.

"All right. Take care, dear. And we'll see you in a couple of weeks." She smiles at me like I'm having her grandchildren or something, and I can't help but smile back at her.

I get dressed and thank the nice nurse again as I walk out, though I see the mean one and return the glare she's giving me. I don't know why that woman hates me so much, but I am feeling empowered at the moment for some reason, so I don't mind giving her the stink eye.

I walk back toward my room and see Shelby and Kelly waiting just down the hall from the infirmary. They look nervous, and immediately, a pulse of fear radiates through me.

"Is everything okay?" I ask.

They both nod. "Yes, the Alphas are all okay. Mark and Tristan are on their way back here now, but Reece and Eli will take a bit longer," Kelly explains.

I have a feeling they're not telling me everything, but I don't say more. "Okay. Why do you both look so pale and bothered?"

Shelby clears her throat. "King Gene was looking for you a few moments ago," she explains. "And I think he may be waiting for you in your room."

I feel my pulse begin to race as I reach them, and Shelby takes my hand. "Why?" I ask.

'We don't know. He wouldn't say, and Adam didn't know," Shelby replies.

"Where's Emily?" I ask. What if she's in there, too? What if he intends to hold me down while she stabs me through the heart with one of her stilettos?

"I think she's gone from the castle," Kelly explains. "Eli said that they'd sent her away with Alpha Stephen."

"Well, what if she came back?" I question.

"We won't let anything happen to you," Kelly assures me.

I want to believe her, but we're talking about two women and a pregnant lady who is already so big, I look like I swallowed a watermelon, versus a king and his bitch cousin who is dead set on killing me.

No, I don't feel good at all.

When we reach my room, both ladies accompany me inside. I see King Gene sitting in the chair I normally sit in by the window, and it's clear to me that he's alone. If Emily were here, I'd smell her perfume. The king doesn't even look over at us as we come in.

"It's about time you got back," he mutters. "You waddle like a fucking penguin."

"She's pregnant, Your Majesty," Shelby counters, a tone of irritation in her voice.

He turns then, and looking at my friends orders, "Leave. Now."

Both of them hesitate. "It's okay," I reassure them, taking a seat on the edge of my bed. "I'll be fine."

"We'll be close by," Kelly says, and I almost expect her to hiss at the king. But they both turn and leave, and I am alone with King Gene again, something I truly hate.

"You certainly have gotten bigger since the last time I saw you," he remarks, stating the obvious.

My initial reaction is to tell him he looks shorter, but I say nothing. He is still the king, and none of my Alphas are here at the moment to protect me. I rub my stomach, willing my children to be safe from this evil man and reply, "How may I help you, Your Majesty?"

King Gene's smile spreads across his face, the note of evil infused in it seeming to spread as well. "You know, you'll be popping out those babies soon. In just a few short months, they'll be crawling from your womb. Then... there will be no need for you in my castle anymore."

I let the idea that he probably thinks that the babies will crawl out of me go, and nod my head. "Yes, Your Majesty, I am aware that once the babies are born, you think there will be no reason to keep me. But, I would like to humbly remind you that all children need their mother–not just any mother, but their own birth mother. They are smart enough to know the difference between any old woman who is just stepping in and their actual mother."

He stares at me for a moment, like he's not sure if what I'm telling him is the truth. "Well, these children will be babies still. And babies are dumb."

I don't know what he thinks I was trying to say. Babies are smart enough to know their mother, and that is the truth. I shake my head. "These babies will take after their fathers and be very smart."

He swallows hard, like he hadn't taken into account the fact that I will be needed still. He shakes his head. "I will not continue to tolerate you after the children are born. Hopefully, you will die while they are crawling out of you. But if you don't, well, just don't get too comfortable here, Breeder."

Not wanting him to see that he's gotten to me, I take a deep breath and ask him, "Where is your cousin, Emily? I haven't seen her around recently."

His gaze narrows on me. "Not here." That's all he says, and I know he won't say more, so I don't press him.

He stands now, and we are almost even in height with me sitting on the bed and him actually pulling his shoulders back and jutting his chin up. "Don't get cozy."

With that, he turns and walks out of my room, leaving me all alone.

But it doesn't last long. Shelby and Kelly run into the room a few seconds later, and I am happy to see that Mark and Tristan are with them.

I'm not sure who to hug first, so I hug both of them. "What's going on?" I ask. "Where have you guys been?"

"There was a minor problem back at your own pack," Mark admits, and I know that he's trying to be nonchalant. "But we took care of it."

"And your parents are fine," Tristan tells me, though he's snarling almost as much as King Gene with the words, and I know he has met them.

"They're lovely, aren't they?" I ask, but he just shakes his head. "Where are Reece and Eli?"

"We were afraid Alpha Stephen might not be done with his tricks, so they stayed behind. We wanted to make sure the people in your village are safe since we assume that you care about them, but we also wanted to make sure that you were safe as well."

"I'm fine," I assure them. I'm glad that they are taking care of my pack despite my parents. Continuing, I say, "I don't think that Emily is here."

"She's not," Mark assures me as he smooths back my hair. "But that doesn't mean she's not a threat anymore."

"And knowing King Gene, he's not done with his shenanigans," Tristan adds with an ominous tone.

A shiver goes down my spine as I figure he is probably right.

Gene

Back in my office, I think about that stupid bitch's words, and I realize, without Emily here, I still need a Luna. I still need those bastard children to have a mother. I still need a queen.

Emily is not royalty material. She's proven that to me time and time again. No, I need a strong woman, a smart woman, one who can meet these Alphas where they are.

I pull out my laminated guide to who is who in the kingdom and flip through. After a few minutes, my eyes settle on a beautiful face, and a smile curls up my lips.

I pick up the phone and begin to dial. A moment later, a feminine voice on the other end greets, "Shore pack. How may I help you?"

"Yes," I say, thoughts racing in my head. "This is King Gene. I want to speak to Luna Barbara. Now."

CHAPTER 32: UNDER ATTACK

Tristan

A commotion outside causes me to pause with my coffee mug halfway to my mouth. I gaze over at Mark, who looks at me with a similarly perplexed gaze.

"What is happening out there? What's that noise?" I ask as I strain my ears to listen to what a voice from outside is saying.

All I can make out is a female voice saying something about the capital. I put my mug down a little too hard and some coffee spills out. I don't care about the mess and head out the door of the dining hall. Mark follows close behind me as we make our way to where the commotion is coming from.

"Oh, you're not so tough now are you, King Gene? I thought you were the almighty king, but it seems you're just a delusional piece of royal ass. Guess who got power over the capital? We do! We do! And we did this right under your nose. All powerful royal army my bouncy ass," a woman exclaims as she walks up and down the stairs leading into the main hall.

"Who is that?" Mark asks me.

I shrug. The woman is tall and slim with midnight black hair that flows down to just above her butt. The long flowy black dress she's wearing gives the appearance of a rebellious gothic flare. As we stand and look at her, she turns and eyes us with a look just as black as her hair, her eyes fixated on us.

"Oh, if it's not the famous Alphas. Where were you when we were taking over the capital? I thought you were the strongest and most feared around these parts. I wonder why either of you would even be considered for the role of king.... Seeing as a similarly incompetent jerk nominated you, why am I even surprised?"

"You will not speak so disrespectfully of your king!" Mark shouts at her.

We advance toward the woman, and she looks at us and sneers. "Whose king? Do you mean short stuff in there? You really still think he's king after I've just told you that we have taken charge of the capital?"

I frown. Who is this woman and who is 'we'? Had Stephen somehow come back and attacked the capital? Or is she Alpha Kane's messenger?

The woman seems like she's not making any effort to get away from us as we get closer to her. I would expect her to have made a run for the woods by now. It's either she has guts, is stupid, or desires to die.

When we are a few feet from her, she runs in the opposite direction before pathetically tripping over her feet and tumbling to the ground. She throws her hands up and waves them with so much exaggeration and cries out, "Oh, no. I fell."

This is the worst acting I have seen since my high school drama club days. What is this crazy lady's deal? We catch up to her fallen form and force her to her feet.

"Oh, aren't you both gentlemen? How dare you manhandle a woman?"

I frown as we half drag her into the castle. This whole display seems like a play straight out of an 'Acting for Dummies' book. As we take her to King Gene, she doesn't put up any struggle.

The king is pacing up and down the war room when we get there with the woman.

"This lady was in the front yard claiming to have taken control of the capital," Mark announces.

The king looks at the woman and frowns. "I heard someone attacked the capital. I had no idea Luna Barbara was behind the attack. Why do you come here? Why did you attack the capital? Who sent you?"

Again, I can't help but frown. The king seems to be reading from a poorly written script of his own.

"No one sent me. I just wanted everyone to see how poorly you are doing as a king. People shouldn't relax thinking they are safe. You're so pathetic," Luna Barbara spits.

I look from the king to this Luna Barbara. Something feels off.

"We'll throw her in the dungeon until we decide what to do with her," I explain as I turn to drag her toward the dungeon.

"Wait. Luna Barbara can't be thrown in the dungeon. Erm, she is very important and could prove very useful for my, erm, fight against Kane," King Gene counters.

Again I turn to look at him. What is going on here?

"How would she be useful against Kane's army? Do you want to use her as bait or something? Does the old man Kane have a weakness for malnourished women?" I ask.

The king runs his hand through his hair. I can't help but think he is trying to cook up some elaborate lie and is buying time.

"Her pack is powerful; we could do a trade with them, yes. We will tell them to give us some of their strongest men in exchange for her release. We could do with more fighters," he suggests.

"Is that so?" I muse. "Why can't you just command them if you're their Alpha King?"

He just glares at me, not answering.

"So what do we do with her?" Mark asks.

I look at him, wondering if he is sensing how odd this whole thing sounds.

"I have a collar with me here. We will allow her to roam the castle with the collar on. I will use the collar to track her movements to make sure she can't escape," King Gene explains.

He takes out a blue collar from his desk drawer and brings it to where we stand, still grasping Luna Barbara. He tries to stand on his tippy toes to reach her neck but fails. I shake my head and let go of Luna Barbara knowing Mark still has her in his grasp. I pick up the king like a little boy and lift him up. After he fastens the collar around her neck, I place him back down.

My eyes keep going to the collar, and I frown. "Isn't that a dog collar? How are we to keep track of her with a dog collar on? Is she going to be on a leash? I don't see any trackers."

"I got it from Emily's toy box a while ago. It has a GPS tracking system, it's just super small, and the collar is not so easy to remove," he clarifies, attempting to make his case.

"You mean its click-on buckle is really that difficult to remove? I guess since a dog can't remove it, Luna Barbara here won't be able to remove it either. She does seem like a bitch. I'm waiting for a hidden camera crew to jump out and yell, 'Cut, you've just been pranked.'" I don't bother to mask the sarcasm in my voice.

The king looks at me, a look of intimidation and defiance in his eyes. "Do you dare to question my word?"

"Not at all. I mean, you know Luna Barbara better than any of us. If you say she can't take off a dog collar on her own, I believe you. She couldn't even run away when she tried, so who knows?" I reply.

I wonder if Mark is buying this whole act. Something seems unusual about this whole arrangement.

LATER, in the shower, I lather my hair for the third time as I try to digest everything that happened today. A woman who launched a supposed attack on the capital is roaming free around the castle, with a dog collar on. Had my life switched from reality to some sort of elaborate prank show?

I dry myself from my shower and walk back into my room with a huge towel wrapped around my waist. When I get into my room, I freeze. Luna Barbara is standing near my bookshelf wearing one of

THREATS AGAINST THE BREEDER

the maid costumes I keep in my party closet. The maid costume is so short that half her ass is hanging out of it.

She is fake-dusting my room with the feather duster that goes with the outfit. When she sees me, she bends over. I realize that she isn't wearing any underwear.

"What the hell are you doing in my room?" I ask as I avert my gaze from her bare bottom.

"Oh, I didn't see you there. King Gene decided to punish my bad-bad behavior with some hard labor. He said good behavior is rewarded." She bats her eyelashes at me and smiles at me suggestively.

What in the royal Emily Part Two is this?

CHAPTER 33: CAUSING TROUBLE

Tristan

I open my mouth and close it again. Luna Barbara is again cleaning the imaginary dust in my room, humming as she does so and swaying her hips. 'Is this woman high on something?' I wonder. I'm about to tell her to get out when there's a knock at the door.

I need to put on some clothes, so I grab a pair of jeans and try to put them on underneath the towel. I can see Luna Barbara looking at me from the corner of her eye and giggling.

I open the door to find Mark standing there. I step out into the hall in just my jeans and no shirt.

"Did you get the memo that we now have a new chambermaid?" I ask.

His brows fuse together in confusion. "Why would we need a new chambermaid?" he asks.

"Luna Barbara is in my room cleaning right now. She is wearing the maid Giggle's outfit," I explain.

"Who is Giggle?" Mark inquires.

"Some maid outfit I keep for role-playing nights. The outfit comes with a feather duster, so when we play, my partner gets to use the duster on my body… tickle me and such. So Giggle it is," I explain.

Mark nods, but I can see the look of amusement on his face. "Sometimes just when I start to think you're normal.... Is that why you're shirtless? Was Giggle going to work on you, tickling your biceps and all?"

I look down at my naked upper body. "No, no. I found her in my room as I came out of the shower. Couldn't even get to my clothes, so I just grabbed the nearest pair of jeans. She's blocking the way to the closet."

Mark folds his arms across his chest and shakes his head. "What is her deal?"

"I have no idea. I think there's something amiss about this whole thing. Why is King Gene allowing her to roam around the palace freely? That thing he put on her is a dog collar. GPS, my male pedicured foot! I'm the king of gadgets, and that's just a plain old collar for a house pet," I declare.

"So, what do you think is going on? Could she have been sent here by Emily?" Mark asks.

I scratch my chin as I try to make sense of everything. "Umm, did you find out anything about the capital attack?"

"Yes. I hear some shifters did go and cause a lot of havoc there. No one was injured; they just destroyed some market stalls and damaged a few building windows. By the time the royal guards got there, the shifters were gone," Mark explains.

"Maybe the attack was just a ploy for her to interject herself in here. The question is why," I remark.

"I hear she's the leader of Shore Pack," Mark offers.

"Where is her husband? Could he be another Alpha who wants to become the next king and has sent her here to infiltrate the castle?"

"No husband. She was married, but her husband died. She took on the role of Luna with ease, so I doubt she is as dull as her acting a few hours ago. Her pack respects and fears her. The pack is also very powerful. Best Luna out there, and she has made the pack greater than when her late husband ruled," Mark reports.

I scratch my head as I let Mark's information sink in. "Do you think she's dangerous? Could she be here to hurt Rose so that she becomes queen instead? Maybe we should make Reece and Eli aware of the new development in case we need them back here," I propose.

"Besides causing a little damage to the capital, bad acting, and cleaning your room, I doubt she's as big a threat to Rose's well-being as Emily was. Nothing in her history points to her being a psychotic murderer. Telling the others about her will just cause unnecessary panic. We need them focused fully on the battle with Stephen," Mark reasons.

I nod. "But she'll try to seduce one of us since I suspect she does have her eye on the queen's title. She's already acting like Emily in that regard. The maid outfit leaves little to the imagination, I can assure you," I explain. I purposefully don't tell him that she's not wearing anything underneath the skimpy skirt. I think that telling him that I'd caught a glimpse of her bleached butt crack would just be admitting that my eyes had somehow cheated on Rose.

"None of us is going to fall for any seductress. Rose is the only woman we need. Not even fifty or sixty women can change that," Mark points out.

"That's a fact I can't dispute. She is everything and more than any man could ever need. I mean she managed to tame me…. She did that without even trying," I say.

I hear a familiar buzzing sound and then a small moan coming from the closed door behind me.

"Oh, no she didn't," I groan as I open the door and dash back into my room.

I can hear Mark's footsteps walk away from the door, probably leaving me to deal with this woman. I don't blame him; he'd once had to deal with a similar incident of his own with Emily.

My heart is still racing as I shut the door behind me. Luna Barbara is stretched out on my bed with a silly grin on her face.

She lets her hands wander over her body, never taking her eyes off me, first teasing her nipples through the thin cotton material of the maid outfit, then moving down her flat tummy. She lets her fingers find the bottom hem of the outfit and pull it up slowly. I hear a moan escape her lips as she slips her hand into her glistening intimate folds.

Her fingers run over her swollen clit, and I watch as her body quivers. She begins to make light circles around her folds, making sure to tease the opening with her middle finger. Luna Barbara moans again. I watch her quicken the pace with her fingers, changing between rubbing her nub and slipping her middle finger into her shaved beaver and squeezing her thighs against it.

She smiles softly at me and licks her lips as she slides her hand out and grabs the magic wand vibrating next to her. I can't move, as if someone has cast a freezing spell on me.

Luna Barbara traces the vibrator around her covered breasts; her hips are already squirming against the bed. She brings the wand to her exposed mound. As it grazes her clit, she throws her head back and moans loudly. She grabs her breast with her free hand as she lets the wand slide up and down the length of her innermost lips.

She slips the wand into her cave and moans, long and soft. She grips the wand tightly as she pushes it further in, almost the entire length. She begins to rock her hips as she licks her lips, her eyes trained on me.

As I watch her, my mind replays the night I used the magic wand on Rose. Her eyes were not so haunted as the woman splayed before me. They were full of wonder and an appreciation that melted my heart, making me want to please her even more. Her cries were not cocky and exaggerated like this woman's. They were full of desire and love. Rose's moans call out to me, not repel me like this.

I taste the bile rise in the back of my throat. I walk over to her and grab the wand. "No one touches or uses my magic wand, except for me and Rose. Now get your slimy coochie off my bed and get out!"

She blinks at me, a look of shock on her face.

"But weren't you enjoying the show?" Luna Barbara blinks up at me.

"Maybe a little more practice would help you. My woman could teach you a thing or two. Then maybe you could use what you learn on your own man. Now get out. I need to sanitize my magic wand. Who knows what has been inside that devil's cave of yours?"

She opens her mouth and then closes it. She gets up, straightens the maid's uniform, and leaves without another word.

I take out some sanitizer and start cleaning the wand. "I'm so sorry I let it get that far. You and I belong to Rose. Oh, my sweet, sweet Rose. Forgive me for watching her use my magic wand for so long without stopping her," I say to the empty room.

I feel like I let the love of my life down, and I can feel angry tears burning my eyelids. I find myself wishing this same sanitizer could clean my eyes from the disgusting sinful act I have just seen.

Banter of the Devil (coming soon)

The Mafia Kings series

Indebted to the Mafia King

Loved by the Mafia King (releases 9/15/2024)

Sign up for Bella's newsletter here.

Follow Bella on Facebook here.